Alicia Cahala

C000056407

THE FAERIES OF FABLE ISLAND

ALICIA CAHALANE LEWIS is a ninth-generation Quaker from the Shenandoah Valley of Virginia. She holds an MFA in creative writing from Naropa University where her poetry appeared in *Not Enough Night*. She is the author of the prose poem *nebulous beginnings and strings* featuring art by Shenandoah Valley artist Winslow McCagg (Tattered Press, 2017). Her chapbook, *The Fish Turned the Waters Over so the Birds Would Have a Sky*, a contemplative meditation on the origins of evolution, was published by The Lune Chapbook Series (Spring, 2017). *The Intrepid Meditator* (2021), a self-help memoir, and the novellas, *Room Service Please* (2022) and *Restless* (2023), were published by Tattered Script Publishing. An excerpt from *Fable Island* will be published by Tattered Script Publishing (2024). A Reiki Master and meditation teacher, Alicia continues to live and work in the Shenandoah Valley.

aliciacahalanelewis.com

Also by

ALICIA CAHALANE LEWIS

The Intrepid Meditator: Connecting Soul to Self

Room Service Please

Restless

THE FAERIES OF FABLE ISLAND

The Faeries Of Fable Island

Alicia Cahalane Lewis

Tattered Script Publishing

Tattered Script Publishing
PO Box 1704
Middleburg, Virginia 20117
tatteredscript.com

ISBN 978-1-7375219-6-9
eISBN 978-1-7375219-7-6
Printed in the United States of America
10 9 8 7 6 5 4 3 2 1

Tattered Script Publishing: Crafting Cultural Creativity and Authenticity

Cover art by J. Felice Boucher
Cover design by Emily Kallick

First Printing, 2024

For my grandchildren, Emi Cahalane and Jago Robbie, with love

One

Secluded throughout all time as though the very nature of its existence would be in jeopardy if it was ever found, Fable Island rests, as all good islands of its kind rest, in the imaginations of those who believe in the faerie realm. This is to say that only those with imaginations of a certain aptitude know that a faerie realm exists. Without them, ordinary people like you and me would go about exploiting our natural resources, each other, and what is good. I don't think I believe in the faerie part, but I do believe we should be better stewards of our planet. So why, after over a hundred and thirty years of collective speculation and uncertainty around the globe, am I the one to see the island, long ago forgotten or dismissed as imaginary, lifting itself off the watery horizon like a rising sun?

I close my eyes and count 1-2-3. When I open them, and the island is still there, I close them again and count 1-2-3-4-5. I open them once more to see that the island is still in view and is lifting itself out of the water like a phoenix rising from the ashes. I can't help but laugh. That's a cliché. There are no phoenixes. Certainly, there are no imaginary islands that suddenly become real. These are myths. I close my eyes against the early morning sun and recite my mother's prayer. "Please heavenly angels, grant me the safety of mind and the security of the ground below my feet so that I may walk about my day without fear."

I open my eyes again, dig my toes into the coarse sand at the edge of the water, and scrutinize the horizon. The island remains. I turn to look behind me but the rocky Maine beach is empty. There is no one here to verify if what I am seeing is real. I fold my hands over my eyes like a pioneer coming across a mirage in the American West. Perhaps she sees a lone oak or an abandoned homestead that might offer a bit of shade, a respite, a glass of sherry, or a comfortable chair to sit upon as she passes through another foreboding territory on her way to someplace grand. I stare at the island still emerging from the gray waves and imagine myself as a pioneer on such a journey. I would do well as a lone traveler, I think. I have no one. I am alone.

I smile, hesitantly, as though this is all some distant memory. A tall tale. A long-told story. I would do well as a lone traveler until I would need a comforting glass of sherry. Isn't that what all fine ladies traveling across the dusty West over a hundred and fifty years ago would have wanted? I throw a pebble into the choppy water and curse my mom for telling me these stories. "I'm not some helpless woman, Mom. Geez. You weren't either. Why did you make me pretend that we were?"

I pick up a handful of small round pebbles and chuck them into the waves. "Dressing me up in your antique clothes and serving me all those glasses of lavender tea in your chipped crystal goblets. Answer me. Why were we always pretending that Fable Island was real? It's not real Mom. It never was. Ever!" I turn from the apparition. "You're gone from me, Mom. So go," I cry, stumbling on the slippery beach stones. "Stop haunting me."

The beach consists of chestnut-colored pebbles that have yet to be pulverized into sand by the endless motion of water moving them back and forth. They are still round like our planet turning itself in circles year after year. I imagine them moving in unison like a school of minnows as the ocean waves push them about this way and then that, as our planet moves us around the sun and then around again.

The waves are angry today. They hit my shins and then my thighs until I step quickly out of the way. My blue jeans are getting soaked. I'm not an idiot. I know I shouldn't stay in the water, but I no longer feel smart as the cold burns like a fire inside of me, daring me to dive under the turbulence. It is but another one of those painful moments that come on without warning when I think about entering the water and leaving this world behind. I pull back from the waves, panicked. I would never do that! But something isn't right. I know it. I turn away from the island and curse my mother and father for putting fairy tale ideas into my head. There are no fairy tales. No imaginary islands. No Faerie Queen. No Peter Pan. But when I think about my mom, I think of Fable Island. I can't help it. I push my way over the uneven ground and trip. "Go. I don't need you, Mom. Stop getting into my head."

There must be hundreds of thousands of these granite pebbles strewn across our rugged beach, which is located much farther north than the soft sands and calm turquoise waters of the Caribbean. The stones push up against jagged granite boulders, these mottled gray and oversized angular jewels, that once escaped from a dark pine forest and tumbled down to the sea. The ground is littered with ribbons of dried ink-colored seaweed and rotting logs carried up onto the beach during the many fierce high tides. They have never been retrieved by clawing waves during the many reoccurring storms, so as a part of some forgotten land they, too, live on this beach as a lasting reminder of all that is dead.

I glance toward the island praying to some mythical god that it won't be there, but it is. It's not supposed to be there. There's no reason for it to be. We don't know for certain that Fable Island exists for there is no proof, no confirmation, and no photograph. It doesn't appear on any map because it exists only in the imaginations of those who believe in a faerie realm. There. I have said all that I need to say. There is no island. There is no faerie realm. There is no story. "There's no going back and putting something to right, Mom," I shout. "You died and left me! Dad abandoned me! That's so wrong!"

I can just begin to make out the tall wiry spires from emerald-colored firs jutting out through the mist, but I choke back my words and grimace. I meant fog. Mist belongs in fairy tales. I pull my hands through my tangled hair and shout, "Is anyone seeing this? Hello? What is happening to me?"

The lonely shrill of a black-legged kittiwake, calling *kittee-wa-aaake, kittee-wa-aaake,* echoes across the open water, but when the gull soars stately out of view, there is silence. Except there isn't silence. There is the discordant pull of agitated waves along the coarse sand, and as each wave comes ashore and slaps the ground, the worn pebbles turn over and onto one another. I close my eyes and listen. Ruptured chords of somber pebbled notes repeatedly strike the ground. They reverberate like a pentatonic piano scale. Not only can I hear the waves crash in my ears, but I can hear them within every cell of my body.

Did you know that our cells can hear? They don't hear in the same way our ears can hear, so to use the word "hear" isn't quite right, but neither is it wrong. We don't have a word to describe just how our cells hear outside noises, thoughts, or bodily functions, but according to my dad, this is why we no longer live in harmony with Earth. We don't give our bodies permission to listen. Was he right? I have no idea. He was always high on some idea or another. He did make a very good argument that our bodies are designed to respond to our environment, but as I stand here now remembering him, I can't help but think that for most of the short time he was in my life, he filled my brain with nonsense.

Mom died ten years ago today, on March 3, 2014. In his grief, or maybe it was just his messed up mind that made him do it, Dad bolted three days later. I had just turned six years old when he left me behind. A lot has happened in these last ten years, and not much of it has been good. I live with my aunt Georgia, Mom's younger sister, and well, as I said, not much about any of it has been good. If I'm being honest, I'd say it's been shit.

I was probably two or three years old when Dad started filling my head with lies about Fable Island. Of course, I don't remember everything he told me then, but by the time I was six and could begin to recognize the truth, I realized I was being sold a pretty lame story. After all, no one could prove the island existed, so of course, I thought it was fake. But like my dad, maybe I thought somewhere deep within my reverberating body there was this possibility. That's probably what I remember most about being a child. The story. The hope. The probability that one day, because for five generations our family had believed more than anyone else in the potential of Fable Island, we would be the ones to see it.

I remember coming down to the beach to watch the tourists who came looking for the island. They would clip their big black cameras onto tripods, balance them on the shifting stones, and peer through their telescopic lenses. Dad said they came here from all over the world, and every once in a while, we would hear an excited, "There it is!" But one glance in the direction of a pointed finger and the cry would be followed by a chorus of disappointed sighs. Dad called these tourists, with their large extended families all huddled together under their faded beach umbrellas, the Leftovers. To them, Fable Island wasn't a lie. It belonged. It was real. But we weren't like them, he would explain. We weren't Leftovers who sat around hoping for a glimpse of the faerie realm. We didn't hope. We didn't wait. We knew. And because we knew that the magical island was just off the coast, we had a vibration about us, much like the waves that hit the beach, that would make it possible for us to see the faeries first.

As Dad once explained, Fable Island has been and will always be. It is a roving island, never to fade from our minds just because we can't see it. Seeing it and believing in it doesn't have to happen for the truth of Fable Island to be real. Fable Island, to those who didn't reach for it but trusted its existence, would present itself when the time was right. And he was convinced that we would be the ones to see the island because we were the ones who knew not to need it. We were the ones who knew not to wish for it. And this, he promised me, would be the reason why Fable Island would make itself known to me. We didn't hope that Fable Island was real. We knew it to be so.

———

Painfully, I laugh out loud. "I'm not seeing it," I shout to anyone within earshot. But of course, because it's still winter, no one else is here. I turn and look up at the two-story clapboard cottage perched prominently upon the granite hillside. For two stories the battered house is small, the ceilings low, and it sits begrudgingly surrounded by wild thorny rose bushes, overgrown shrubbery, and too-tall pine trees with spindly tops. Sculpted by prevailing winds, the trees are on the verge of toppling. My great-great-grandfather, a ship's captain, built the cottage over one hundred and fifty years ago. The narrow front door faces the open ocean channel because, at the time, people would travel to the house by boat. Now the red-painted door has faded to pink and is bolted shut. We only use the kitchen entrance which has a rickety storm door that slams itself shut every time we open and close it. The white paint on the clapboard siding is peeling, the gray asphalt shingled roof is sagging, and because of the many ocean storms that hit the house, the cottage is listing on its side like a schooner taking on water.

"Do you hear me? I said I'm not seeing the island!" It's getting windier so I pull back my long copper hair and secure it with an elastic band. My ponytail whips around and slaps me in the face. "The Leftovers aren't even here, Dad," I shout annoyed. "There's no one left. No one! Why am I even here? There's nothing left of your promise." I turn my back to the island and curse, "I hate you for leaving me here."

I stumble down the beach going nowhere, turn my back to the wind, and look up at my house. I shouldn't call it "my house." It has never felt like my house but more like a fortress I was forced to move into after my mom died, a lonely forgotten fortress where I have been locked in a garret looking down on a world that moves along without me. I am but one of the many souls destined to be trapped here, I think, retrieving another round stone and chucking it into the water. I fear it is my ancestors' past that haunts me. I don't belong here. I am not like them. I have never been nor do I want to be like my family. "Idiot!" I shriek, cursing my great-great-grandfather. "You should have burned it down when you had the chance. That way no one would know about Fable Island. No one would know anything about the Faerie Queen! Or Peter Pan!"

I cannot reconstruct the past nor put it back the way I want it, and this is what bothers me the most about living in someone else's version of my life. I wasn't supposed to live here. We had a home in town where I lived with my mom and dad. I had a big grassy yard to play in, a swing set, and a chocolate-colored cocker spaniel. Now I have only this vague memory of something happy, but it is far away, veiled in wind and fog. "This will always be a house of dreams," my aunt told me when she moved us here after my father left me. "No," I want to tell her now. "This will never be a house of dreams but a house where dreams go to die."

I turn to look at the island emerging from the waves and shout, "You're not real! Faeries aren't real. Peter Pan is only a figment of someone's imagination!" But the island and the dream and the wind and the veil have returned, and I, Megan Elida Fay, forever forgotten by my mom and dad, am destined to stay trapped in a story someone else wrote for me.

Two

It was back in 1890 when a scholarly, well-traveled, and respected European ornithologist, coming to these rugged parts to study the migratory pattern of finches, first spotted the island emerging through the waves from this very shore. He wrote about this unexplained but curiously appealing experience in a beautiful book entitled *Fable Island*, which at the time created a worldwide sensation, a kind of mass hysteria about the possibility of an actual faerie realm. The book was full of intricately drawn etchings and vivid descriptions of the island. Prof. Ralston Yardley ignited the imaginations of those who were looking for something more meaningful in their over-industrialized lives when he declared that the much sought-after Faerie Queen was real.

Over the last century, hundreds of thousands of people have traveled to this beach in the hope of seeing the island. Many have camped out with their worn and faded copies of *Fable Island*, their rattan picnic hampers, and opera glasses, to glimpse what Prof. Yardley once assured them exists. Fable Island became someplace worth longing for, and my dad, an eager young man just out of college, desiring something romantic and otherworldly, traveled across the Atlantic Ocean from Copenhagen in search of his promised land right here on the coast of Maine.

Prof. Yardley said that traveling to Fable Island would be like traveling to heaven on earth, and I guess Dad convinced himself that this kind of heaven was just about perfect, because when Mom was sick with breast cancer, anything this Prof. Yardley once promised, and anything my dad could promise that would give her a life worth sticking around for, would be worth finding. She wasn't going to die if we could live on Fable Island. But my dad promised an unrealistic fairy tale, so no, I know I'm not seeing Fable Island. It's impossible. No one has ever been able to prove that Fable Island exists. No one.

"Dad, you never should have made promises you couldn't keep," I hiss, turning to go. I clamber over the wet stones in my bare feet and toss the tangled hair out of my eyes. With my back to the horizon, I continue hopping across the beach in my frozen blue jeans until I'm certain I can let out a long steady breath. "You're such an idiot, Meg!" I shout. "When have you ever believed in fairy tales?"

Shivering from the cold, I throw myself down onto a fraying blue towel, and while still refusing to look up at what I know is nothing, I wrap it around my chafed feet. Fragments of stone dust and mica cling to my skin. Shake it off, I tell myself. Shake off the illusion of the Faerie Queen and get out of here. But the pull of this once-famous beach is real, of that I am certain. I know it is my mom who is the one doing the pulling. She comes to me at times and asks me to remember her. And then I do.

She's not real anymore. At least she's not flesh and bones real, but then again, she's not not real. I imagine her spirit tumbling about like a pebble across the universe turning over and over and round and round. Ever since the day she died, it feels like I can hear her. I don't hear her with my ears, but if I listen I feel her speak to me with my heart. I'm sure it was her idea that I come down to the beach this morning. I'll never tell anyone this, but this way, if I let myself believe that I can hear her, she won't really be gone. I refuse to look at the island. I won't. "You can go now, Mom," I say exhaling. "I'm fine. Please, go."

I close my eyes and remember her vivid copper hair and her dimpled smile. Mom was like a colorful illustration, all citrine and turquoise and indigo until cancer took the flush from her cheeks and the color from her lips. She has become stuck in my mind as these two distinctly different versions of herself. I like the colorful version best, but I am no longer a child and I know what real life is like. I know that death comes whether or not we are ready for it. I can still hear Georgia's insipid voice in my head. "It's simply the way things are, Meg. We're organisms destined to die."

There I was, six years old, having learned from my mom and dad these abstract notions that time is nebulous, loss is inevitable, and Fable Island is real. I can still remember how they insisted we respect Earth, for if we harmed Earth we would harm the Faerie Queen. Should we hurt the queen we, in turn, would hurt ourselves for Earth and the queen are one. I was taught that Fable Island would help those who sought to understand the microscopic level of complexities the world had to offer and that the Faerie Queen held the answers to all that had been misconstrued about our stewardship. In truth, it wasn't a normal childhood.

I can't help but shout, "I know we're destined to die, Mom, but then why should we live?" I shake my head in disbelief as the tears begin to fall. I will keep my head down. I won't look. I know the island isn't there. How can it be? It's not real. And I know I won't see Mom. She's gone. I wipe my nose on the sleeve of my sweatshirt and run my hands down my pink cheeks.

I'm pretty sure it is my six-year-old self that misses my mom the most and this is why I came down here on the anniversary of her death looking for the bridge to Fable Island that she promised I would one day find. But of course, it's not possible. I will be sixteen tomorrow, old enough to know there isn't a bridge. There was never an island. I don't believe in fairy tales. I look up, hesitantly, half expecting, half wishing the island to be there, but it's gone. As I knew it would be. As it should be.

Three

"Time heals all wounds," says Georgia, quickly rummaging around my attic room for a pair of dry socks. "Here. Put these on," she says, shaking them in front of my face. "You shouldn't be down at the beach without your boots. Not on a day like this." She looks at me and shouts, "It's 35 degrees out there, Meg! What were you thinking?" I want to tell her about the island, but she covers me in one of her crocheted blankets insisting that I think smarter. I'm so cold I'm shaking. I am not smarter. If anything, I think I'm forgetting everything she ever taught me about staying safe.

"Those are too small," I complain, tossing the socks onto the bed.

Georgia isn't listening. She never does. "Well," she says, shoving the childish white socks with scalloped lace ruffles onto my feet, "you were thinking with your heart and not with your head. And the heart…"

I pull off the socks. "No. I was thinking."

"Well, you can't skip school every time you feel this way."

"But if I don't go down there…"

Looking me over from head to toe, Georgia says, "What's really going on, Meg? You're going down there more and more often."

"It was ten years ago today."

"I know what day it is."

"Mom died ten years ago. Today. I had to go."

"Ten years is a long time..."

"But you just said time heals all wounds."

"I said...I don't know what I said. I said you can't keep this up. Skipping school when you feel sad. That won't bring her back."

"You said time heals all wounds. Does it?"

She looks me in the eye. "Yes. It does."

I'm thinking about the bridge to Fable Island. "How much longer?"

Georgia takes two colorful mismatched socks from my dresser drawer, kneels on the floor in front of me, and slips them onto my feet. One sock is black with red stitching, and the other one is cobalt blue with white snowflakes. "Here. Let's put these on. You can't be splashing around down at the beach in your bare feet this time of year. You have no sense when it comes to these things."

"I'm not a child," I complain.

She pushes herself up off the floor, returns her hands to her hips, and looks down at me. "Well, did you see it?"

I look at her and frown. "See what?"

"The bridge."

My eyes widen. "What bridge?"

"You're almost the age when your mother told you that you would see it. So, did you?"

I toss the warm blanket aside and stand abruptly. "She didn't tell me I would see a..."

"She told you the day before she died that you would see the bridge. You're getting to be about the age when she thought you might."

I turn from her and look out the attic window at the desolate beach, but the panes of glass are clouded with condensation and obstruct the view. "I don't know what you're talking about," I lie.

"You know your mother crossed the bridge to Fable Island."

I turn away from the window. "No, I don't."

Georgia is careful not to take her eyes off of me. "I remember the day it happened. The exact time. And what I was wearing," she says. "It was your mother's sixteenth birthday. I was in the sixth grade and I'd just stepped off the bus when she ran up the hill to tell me. Right up there on our gravel drive," she says pointing. "I was wearing a pair of my mother's faded bell-bottoms, her suede clogs, and my grandmother's organza blouse. Do you remember the one? It's hanging in your closet. Well, I didn't want to believe her and have my friends make fun of me so I played it cool and laughed alongside them, but of course, I believed her. She was my older sister. I never would have doubted her."

I'm angry. "What are you talking about? What bridge?"

She looks bewildered for a moment. Of course, I know about the bridge. It's all everyone in our small town ever hoped for. We even had coloring contests at school to see who could create the most magical-looking bridge to Fable Island, but I wasn't allowed to play. Dad said it wouldn't have been fair and

I remember thinking how mean of him. How was I so different that I wouldn't be allowed to enter a stupid coloring contest?

Taking my hands in hers, Georgia continues to study me. "You will be sixteen tomorrow. Imagine that! What would you like for your birthday dinner? I can make you anything you'd like."

"My mother didn't cross a bridge," I insist.

"Pork chops? Lasagna?"

"When? How? You never told me this. She never told me."

"She told you."

"No. I would remember."

"You didn't believe her at the time so maybe you've forgotten, but the way I remember it, your mother..."

"You have only told me repeatedly that when she died she was so sick she didn't even know us. She was unconscious. She wasn't even breathing on her own."

Georgia turns away from me and puts her trembling hand on the cut-glass doorknob. She holds it there for a moment before opening my bedroom door and stepping out of the room. "I'm sorry, Meg. Truly, I am, but ten years is a long time to be wishing her back. She's not gone. You know that. But she's not coming home."

"I know. It's just..."

"It's just becoming impossible to know what to do with you." She looks down at the scuffed wooden floor. "There. I said it. And I don't regret it."

I laugh painfully. "What to do with me?"

She pinches the bridge of her nose with her pointed fingers. "Yes. What to do. You won't go to school when you're sad. And when you do go, you're late. You don't eat. You don't pick up your room. You lie in bed. You don't wash your hair." She raises her voice another octave. "It's wrong. All of it. You know this. And there's nothing more I can do. I've had it, Meg. I've tried. But if you refuse to talk to someone, anyone…a grief counselor, someone at school, a doctor…you're going to live the rest of your life in despair. I don't understand you. You used to be so…"

"I'm OK."

"No. You're not OK. You're living, but you're not OK. You're…"

"What?"

"You're ignoring basic truths."

"That there's a bridge to Fable Island?" I wail. "Mom died ten years ago, Georgia. She haunts me. My father bailed. He's gone. You're my guardian, which neither of us likes. That's the truth."

"Probably," she says, turning her back on me.

"Georgia, I'm sorry. I didn't mean to say that." She quietly descends the narrow attic stairs, taking the crocheted blanket with her. "I'm grateful," I offer, following her. "Lasagna, please. Lots of cheese. No parsley."

When she reaches the bottom step Georgia puts her hand on the faded rose wallpaper and turns to look at me. She traces her trembling fingers over one of the deep gouges on the wall, made at a time ten years ago when she moved a twin bed into the attic for me to sleep on. "Your mother isn't coming back. But the bridge…"

"I don't want to talk about Fable Island. It's not real. I'm fine. Lasagna, please, and I'll help you make it."

She studies me for a moment. "No. You don't have to lift a finger on your birthday. That's your gift. I'll make it."

I smile weakly. "Thank you."

"Invite Theo. It's not a party without her." I nod and Georgia smiles. "Good. Theo likes me."

"That's because you give her anything she wants," I complain. "Including seconds. She's supposed to be on a diet you know…"

"Oh pshaw," says Georgia exhaling. "That child's not fat. It's all in her head."

"You make good lasagna," I admit, doing my best not to ask her about the bridge. "I'll be having seconds."

"OK, that's enough of us propping each other up. Do you want another unexcused absence from school? Is it going to be worth it in the end to fail?"

I look down at the pair of mismatched socks and think about my dad. He failed. "No, I'll go. I have a biology test."

She looks at me and in all seriousness says, "You would do well to take it. Your future depends on it."

Georgia scurries away, thin and nimble like a cat, dressed all in black. Black turtleneck. Black pants. Black Art Deco jewelry. I've never seen her wear anything but black. She tells me that she does it, not because she's in mourning for her sister, but because she's an artist. As if black is supposed to make her better at throwing pots. I turn and climb the steep attic steps on all fours, careful not to slip in my oversized socks. My mom would never have made me sleep in an attic, I think, hauling myself onto the bed and curling into a ball.

I turn toward the patterned wall and count the roses. 1-2-3-4… But I stop. They're not worth counting, going on and on across the wall like stars in the sky. I touch my forefinger to one of the roses and pick at the mottled paper. *"Second star to the right and straight on 'til morning,"* I offer. Sunlight slipping into the room from the only window trips across the shadows and brightens the dark corners. I turn to look under the eaves, for what I don't know, as the light dances playfully along the wall. I can't help but think about Tinker Bell.

"I can't do it, Mom," I try. "I can't go to school today. Maybe I saw an island. I don't know. But I…I didn't see a bridge. Does anyone else know about this?" She doesn't answer. "There are all these noises in my head and they're getting louder. It's not that bad and I think I'm OK and then suddenly I'm not. I'm tipping, Mom. Like the ground is tipping and I have to spend every day trying not to fall." I hit my fist on the wall. "I'm falling, Mom. I can't do this."

The wallpaper is pocked with hundreds of pin holes where I've put up posters, taken them down, and replaced them over the years. I'm staring uneasily at the faded wall because I've recently taken down all the soccer posters. I don't play soccer. Maybe I put them up because I liked the photography. I don't know. I liked something about the camera angles, and how the live action was stopped mid-leap, which made me think about my mom. When her life ended she was caught mid-leap as though somewhere between here and there she was supposed to land and finish out her life being my mom. The wall is a reminder of all that I have lost.

"I'm losing my mind, Mom. I swear to God. Did you tell me when I turn sixteen I'll see a bridge to Fable Island?" Again, she doesn't answer, but I hold my breath and count 1-2-3-4. When she still doesn't answer I roll over and throw myself off the bed. "Fuck this."

My mom died in a hospital bed surrounded by wires and plastic tubing. I was with my dad and Georgia in her beige room when it happened. I don't remember the exact color of the paint, or if it was really beige, but I do remember looking at my freckled skin, looking at the walls, looking at my dad, and then checking the color of his skin. He was not flushed with his usual pink exuberance. Did I know my mom was dying at this exact moment? Probably not. Maybe they told me. Or maybe they were going to wait until they took me home to tell me, but when I left the room with Georgia she told me that my mom was "gone."

I looked up at her and asked, "To Fable Island?" She scooped me up and carried me the rest of the way down the hospital corridor, into the elevator, and out the revolving door.

"You're getting so big," she lied. I wasn't getting big. I was, and still am, small for my age, making it so I'm always mistaken for someone much younger. "Ice cream for you today, my sweet. Peppermint," she chimed. This was Mom's favorite flavor. It wasn't mine nor will it ever be.

———

I open the top drawer of my great-grandmother's oak dresser and rummage through the mismatched socks for the photo album. I've opened and closed it so many times the spine is broken, and the Polaroids under clear plastic sleeves are going blue with age. There's a photo of my grandmother standing in the yard posing next to her yellow '76 Chevrolet Impala. She's wearing a long patchwork skirt she made from some of the old clothes she found in the attic which she cut up and then pieced back together. Her long copper hair is parted on the side and pulled into a barrette. I smile because she looks proud. It was the only car Gramma ever owned and she drove it up until the day she died.

I turn the page. A faded black-and-white photo with white scalloped borders slips out of the album and falls to the floor. I pick it up and tuck it back under the torn plastic cover. It's of my great-grandmother standing in our small kitchen with her long sleeves rolled up and wearing a soiled apron. Her hands are on her hips and she's looking over twenty jars of newly canned pickles.

There's one of my mom and dad on their wedding day. It's hard to tell where the photograph was taken because the image is blurred, but I know they got married where they first met, on the beach overlooking Fable Island. Or what they believed would be their fabled island.

I look at the photograph of Mom holding me when I was a baby. In her arms, I am suspended in time. Her hair covers her shoulders and falls easily down over her breasts. If I could have lifted my newborn arms out of the swaddle I would have touched it.

The scrapbook isn't finished. It, too, lies suspended in time when time was all she had until she was forced, by illness, to reckon with whatever time she had left. I tuck the peeling pink gingham paper borders back under the photo. "I don't look like you, Mom, but I've always wanted to have your beautiful hair and not the mousy version I ended up with. I want to be like you, Mom. I want something. But what?" I close the photo album and shudder. "To believe in magic? No! Fable Island isn't real. How could it be when you're not here to make it real."

Four

Cancer is brutal. There's not a day that goes by when I don't think about it in some way. I don't think about it abstractly like, "My mom had breast cancer and now she's gone." I think about the fact that Mom had all these cancer cells that destroyed her organs. One single cell, the first to go rogue, multiplied and slowly took apart the inside of her body one system at a time. When cancer had pushed the very last breath out of her, that one cell, the first to malfunction, had single-handedly created an entire ecosystem of bad energy in her body. All it took was one mutant cell to ultimately take her life.

"One cell, Theo," I explain.

Theo turns around in her chair and her long dark curls move across my desk like a curtain opening. "Shh…"

I turn my test paper over and slide down in my chair. I'm always the first to finish. "One cell," I whisper.

I close my eyes and imagine the impact of this rogue cell. Without it, my mom and dad would still be here and I wouldn't be living in a garret. We all have cells with damaged DNA, but why do these cells develop into cancer in some people and not in others? Scientists don't fully understand the mechanism despite decades of research. On more than one occasion, Georgia has told me that she thinks Mom died because it was her time. That's her explanation. "She chose her time to go, Meg. She chose this." I don't believe for a second that Mom chose to die and leave me alone like this. She didn't choose death. Death chose her.

"Do you think someone will figure it out?" I whisper.

Theo repositions herself, first one butt cheek and then the other, and leans back in her chair. "Stop obsessing."

"I'm not."

"Shh..." she says, turning her test paper over. "That was brutal."

Death is brutal. I fold my hands in my lap and close my eyes again. In my mind, I am in the passenger seat of Georgia's dented Subaru on my way to school. She was hurrying down the narrow two-lane street anxious to get me to school on time. "Your mother put you first," she squawked, pushing her fringed copper hair out of her eyes. "She didn't leave you on the streets to fend for yourself. She made all the arrangements so that after she left us your father and I..." She turned to me. "Despite the atrocities your father pulled, you know you are well cared for and loved." I turned away from her and looked out the car window at the dirty snowbanks lining the street. "We were both thrown together unexpectedly, but that's what happens sometimes, Meg. Your mother didn't abandon you. Now your father...that's another story."

When Georgia pulled the car around to the front of the old brick building and told me to hop out, she said something I had never heard her say before. I don't know if it was something someone told her to say or if it was her idea, but as I was pushing myself to stand, she said, "You have another year to get your act together, Meg. You're going to need a substantial scholarship. I don't have the money to send you to college. Your father does. Or he did. I don't know where he is or the state of his affairs." I was so taken aback that I turned to her and my backpack slipped off my shoulder and fell to the sidewalk. "This isn't to frighten you, but if you don't want to end up digging trenches for the rest of your life..."

"What's that supposed to mean?"

She lowered her eyes. "Nothing. It was just something our father used to say to us when we were young."

"Grandad?"

"You're late. Go. We'll talk about it tomorrow."

"Tomorrow's my birthday."

"Another day then. Go."

I looked at the crumbling concrete steps and squinted into the sun, eager to turn and run from everything this 1940s building once stood for. Old teachers. Old ideas. Old textbooks. "You don't trust me, do you, Georgia?"

"I never said..."

"I know you think I'm a failure, but I'm not. I'm the smartest one in my class."

Georgia was abrupt. "Then apply yourself and prove it." She leaned over the torn car seat and clawed at the door handle. "Go. And think about what I just said. I'm not sorry," she barked, pulling the rusted door closed. She pushed the car into gear and slowly pulled away, but then she hesitated, as did I. She studied me from the rearview mirror and I could only imagine what she was thinking: "Do I trust Meg to take herself inside or should

I walk with her just to be sure?" There was a moment of inde-
cision on both our parts, but then Georgia stepped on the gas
and the car inched forward. I stood watching to make sure she
would go, but when she stopped and suddenly put the car in
reverse I knew, as I have always known, that Georgia doesn't
know how to trust.

She rolled down the window. "Your mother died, Meg. And
your father abandoned you. That is the cold hard truth. There's
no denying you're still in pain. I get it. I hear you. I see you,"
she said, emphasizing the words, "but if we're going to find our
way out of this we're going to have to do it together. You're too
young..." I lifted my eyes, diverted momentarily to my feet, to
remind her that I was not young, but she continued, "to know
what's best. Too young..."

"Too young to reason?" I shouted.

"Too young to go about your day with your head down in
this continual grief. You're a beautiful child, but you're throwing
away that golden light of happiness with all this despair."

I turned from her and darted across the lawn and away from
the front steps as she struggled to park the car and get out. I will
never go home again, I realized. How can I? Georgia has never,
nor will she ever, see me. Unexpectedly, she caught the sleeve of
my grandmother's crocheted poncho, and panting wildly, pulled
me into her.

"You and I are on the precipice of a monumental decision
here," she wailed. "Either you turn your life around, accept me,
accept that I love you and that we're here to embrace life, or
you will fail." She shook me. "Don't fail me, Meg! For the love
of God, don't fail me too." She pushed me away abruptly, and

as I watched her watching me, perhaps both of us watching for something to break open, tears or more words of anger, I saw this fleeting image of my mother go past me. It happened so suddenly and without warning that I turned from Georgia and gasped.

"Did you see that?" I whispered.

Concerned, Georgia turned to where I was looking. "I didn't see anything."

"It was nothing then," I said alarmed. "I thought I saw..."

"Again?"

"No, not again. Not ever," I shouted. "I don't want to see..."

"Shh," she said, holding onto me. "I don't think you'll be able to make this go away without help. And if it's come to this then it's come to this. And it has." She patted my back awkwardly like the only thing bothering me were hiccups. "We'll get you the help you need."

"But..."

She tightened her grip. "Your mother would not be proud of you right now and that's a fact."

Angrily, I took a step away from her. "How can you be so cruel? I can't help it. I feel what I feel."

"We all feel, Meg. All of us. But how you feel and how you stand and how you dress catapults you deeper into despair. Brush your hair. Put on your smile and go," she said, nudging me toward the door. "Go forward, child. With hope. This cloud you have hovering over you is not pretty."

———

I have thought about death probably more times than Theo, but that's because she hasn't lost. She's gained. Although her mom and dad divorced three years ago, and her dad no longer lives with them, Theo told me that her parents got lonely one night, had sex, and now her mom is expecting a baby. "It's a miracle Mom can still have a baby at her age," said Theo. Her parents aren't getting remarried but plan on raising the baby together. I envy Theo. One cell divides. Two cells divide. Four cells divide. She gains. I lose.

I tap Theo on the shoulder and whisper, "Can you come over after school? I'm not having a good day." She extends her soft plump hand and takes ahold of mine.

It's not my fault, I remind myself. I didn't do anything to cause Mom's death. "Cells go helter-skelter," Grandad once said. He's gone now too, but before he died we spent a lot of time together. When he was feeling lonely and thinking I was probably just as lonely and needed cheering up, he would invite me down to his dusty used bookshop, The Book Galley, and together we would look at his first-edition copy of *Fable Island*. I know he didn't believe that Fable Island was real, but at least he never made anyone feel stupid about it if they did. Certainly, he never made Mom feel stupid. And anyone who came into his shop asking to see the last remaining intact copy of *Fable Island* always got his full attention.

He would put on a pair of pristine white gloves, take the antique book down from a high shelf behind the cash register, lay it down on the distressed wooden counter, and open it with slow deliberate moves. Grandad would peel back the pages one by one as these visitors asked him if he would sell *Fable Island* or donate it to a museum or a library. But Grandad would never part with *Fable Island*. It wasn't his to give away, he would explain. And then he would turn the thin pages as if revealing a secret and show them the illustrations.

He would look down at me standing on the tips of my toes beside him in my dirty tennis shoes and cut-off blue-jean shorts, and remark, "Don't you see the resemblance? This is my granddaughter, Elida Fay. This is her," he would say, pointing to the pen and ink drawing of the Victorian-era faerie with gossamer wings, the one everyone insisted looked like me. And then he would smile easily and explain, "I can't sell *Fable Island*. It belongs to the Faerie Queen."

"My name is Meg," I would remind him.

"Megan Elida Fay," he would sing.

"You know I don't like my name," I would answer.

"Elida is a perfect name. A profound fit for you," he would pronounce. "It means something magical. 'Our little winged one.' Did you know that your name originated in Mexico?"

"Yes, you've told me a hundred times."

Grandad would laugh and say, "I could have sold this old book a hundred times over, you know, 'our little winged one,' and I could have made you a millionaire if your mother hadn't insisted we keep the darn thing." He would then have to explain to these curious seekers that the book was no longer in print and that he didn't know where they could find another copy. They would leave The Book Galley disappointed but glad to have met the Faerie Queen, and together we would smile and tip our heads to them as a Faerie Queen would do, neither haughty nor stuck up, but regal. I was convinced he didn't believe in the faeries of Fable Island. He was just having fun.

When Mom was sent to the hospital for the last time, I cried. We all did because this was, as Georgia said, where she was going to die. As a child, I understood death. I had already lost several goldfish, had watched in distress when they were flushed down the toilet, and I was heartbroken when our cocker spaniel, Daisy, had died. So I knew what I was going to lose, but I had no concept of how long her death would take or how long we would be expected to wait. I would plop down beside Mom on her hospital bed, cross my legs, tuck myself in beside her, and turn the pages of *Fable Island.* I remember complaining about all the tourists who crowded their way into The Book Galley expecting us to know the way to the island. I didn't understand it then, that each day we arrived at her bedside and found her alive was a gift, but each day, at the same time, inevitably brought her closer to death. To a five year old on the cusp of turning six, this kind of time was a distortion.

Mom was too tired to look at the illustrations but she loved it when Grandad read the descriptive passages. She would turn to me, lay a bruised and skeletal hand on mine, and remind me that she had fond memories of the place. Together, Grandad and I would look at one another and smile. We were both old enough to know that his daughter, my mom, loved fairy tales. We didn't want to make her feel any worse than she already did, but no one, aside from my mom and dad, thought Fable Island was real.

I remember when Dad took *Fable Island* from my small hands and pushed the book onto her, begging Mom to fight the cancer so that she could return to the island, assuring her that if she did, all would be well. I remember that his breath smelled sweet like honey, but the way Georgia explained it to me when I got older was like this: "Your father wasn't living in our world, but in his own," she said. "Alcohol is addicting. It hurts the mind." It turns out my dad had a disease that made him see Fable Island through some imaginary distortion. Not unlike time.

Five

A chair scrapes across the classroom floor and I open my eyes. Theo is handing over her test paper. When Ms. Park stands beside me she chirps, "It was an easy test, wasn't it, Meg?" I ignore her. I don't want her to think I found it was easy any more than I want the entire class to think I aced it. I can hear multiple complaints echoing across the room. But it was an easy test. She lays an aging hand on my desk and bends down ever so slightly. "Everything all right?" she asks. I nod uneasily.

She continues shuffling down the row picking up test papers and scanning them before turning back around to look at me. I look down at my feet and her eyes follow. Together we look at the mismatched pair of socks, my grandmother's distressed suede clogs, and the jeans that are just a little too tight and a little too cropped in all the wrong places. Hand-me-downs, all of them.

There are moments in one's life when the body suddenly wakes up. This is one of those moments. I don't remember how many other such moments I have had, because there have been too many to count, but it is at this moment that I realize I'm not dressing like the other girls in my class. Maybe I knew this.

Maybe I go to school not caring about the hand-me-downs, but it is at this precise moment that I realize my blue jeans are not like the ones the other girls are wearing. But then I think, when have I ever cared about being in style? Never. I look up at the girls in front of me, and even though I'm pretty sure they can't afford designer brands, I notice they are all wearing the same style. Some of their jeans are intentionally ripped and faded, and their shirts are cropped, not because they're too small, but because this is the style. When I look down at the torn knees of my jeans and the way Gramma's poncho is starting to unravel, it's easy to tell that my clothes were not manufactured to look cool.

Ms. Park walks past me and puts her hand on my shoulder. "OK, class. Weekend homework...." There is a collective groan and I slide down into my chair so that Ms. Park will remove her hand, but she only tightens her grip. "Go boldly," she says, looking down at me. Theo looks at me, raises her eyebrows in genuine surprise, and smiles. "Go boldly out of this door," continues Ms. Park, lifting her hand from my shoulder and pointing to the classroom door.

Theo asks, "Does that mean we can go?"

"Not yet," she answers. "Take a moment to look around you." She returns her hand to my shoulder. "What do you see?"

I am not the only one who is confused at the moment, but Theo raises her hand and says, "There are twenty-one invertebrate specimens sitting on the table," she says pointing. "They're floating in formaldehyde. Please don't count this test, Ms. Park. I know I failed it."

Ms. Park looks down at me again and grimaces. "And why would I do that, Theo?" I slide farther down into my seat. "There are twenty-two specimens sitting on the table in front of you and not one of them is foreign. We've been talking about them for weeks." She rifles through the test papers one by one and I blush. "I want every one of you to look around this room. What am I seeing?"

There is genuine confusion and Luke says, "The bell's about to ring."

Ms. Park looks at the antique clock on the wall. "I know." She pulls my test paper out from the stack, turns it over, and lays it down on my desk.

Amber complains, "It was a hard test, Ms. Park. I think we all failed it."

Ms. Park looks at the nineteen of us either stooped over our desks eager for the bell to ring, or lying down on them feigning sleep. I close my eyes and pray she doesn't grade my test on the spot and announce the score. "You know what I want?" she says. I open my eyes. Ms. Park pauses and looks again at the clock. It ticks loudly. "In truth, I don't know what I want." I hear a few snickers from the back of the room and Ms. Park responds by making a deep guttural sound in her throat. "I want every one of you to pass this test." A collective groan echoes across the room.

"I won't do this again," she says, looking first at Theo and then at the rest of us, "but consider it my gift to you. Come to class next week prepared to take this test again." There is more complaining, but Ms. Park raises her voice. "There's no reason for anyone in this day and age to fail a test. You're sophomores. You should be old enough and disciplined enough to study. And if you don't, you should be old enough to know the consequences."

Ms. Park taps my shoulder. "And why is it important that you pass? So you can go places. But if you don't want to go anywhere then by all means, fail. The choice is yours. If you genuinely want to try a new life, one that is different from this…" she says, waving her agitated hand, the one holding the test papers, across the room and over toward the window, "then I encourage you to think about why I'm giving you this opportunity to succeed." I hold my breath as she continues. "Theo," she says, pointing to the specimen table, "how many jars are on the table?"

Theo looks down at her desk and winces. "Twenty-two."

"Twenty-two. And not one of you," she continues, tapping my shoulder again, "is prepared for what is about to hit you when you step out of this door on graduation day. Not one of you. You may have it in your thick heads that you're in an insignificant school too run down to amount to much in this working-class town, but just because you're not expected to go places, not expected to leave, and not expected to do anything different from what your older brothers and sisters or your parents did for that matter, doesn't mean that you can't. I don't care if you pass. I genuinely don't care. I will fail you. And you will repeat this class. The choice is yours."

She pulls back her shoulders, crosses the room in a pair of scuffed cognac loafers, and tosses the rest of the test papers into a dented metal trash can. "All it took was one glance at these for me to see that you don't care. I don't know why you don't care, but I expect you to return on Monday with a better attitude toward your future. Now go."

I fold my test paper in half and then in half again, and stuff it into my fraying backpack. Eagerly, everyone unfurls themselves from their desk chairs and sprints for the door, but Ms. Park motions for me to step to the front of the classroom.

"If you come in late again, Meg, I will fail you too." I am genuinely shocked and I open my mouth to speak, but she cuts me off. "Go. I've said everything I need to say. You're just as guilty of apathy as the rest of them."

"But…"

"No," she interrupts, lifting a shaking palm to the ceiling. "How many second chances do you expect to get in one life?" I blush. "One. If you're lucky. So take this as a warning. I didn't grow up with much, Meg. In fact, I grew up with a lot less. Much less. My father was a stevedore working the docks in Portland. A long time ago." She studies me carefully. "He worked hard and made a life for my mother and me that was beautiful," she says. "You have your wits. Use them. I don't want to hear another excuse. You can choose to be late and fail or you can choose to get out of bed, come to school on time, and succeed."

I won't cry, I promise myself, taking a step toward the door. "Poor as a church mouse, my father," she says suddenly. "But he knew that the only way to succeed in life was to laugh," she says, smiling while remembering her father, "and forgive. You have to forgive your father and make your life your own. Do you understand? You're making your life all about him. Make it about you, Meg." I turn from the door and look into her blue eyes. They are watery and she dabs at them with a used tissue. "Poor without the privileges you kids selfishly expect, but that man got more out of his life because of his positive attitude." She motions toward the twenty-two jars lined up on the steel table. "Well done. Not a single mistake. You got them all right." She smiles as she folds her thin hands in front of her chest. "I will say a prayer for you, Meg. For a scholarship. For something. Anything that will get you out of here and on to someplace where you belong."

"But I like it here. I..."

She points a brittle fingernail toward the door. "Go to class."

"But.."

"So poor," she says, remembering. She turns to me and purses her lips. "You don't need your twenty-first-century privileges to get ahead, but you do need to come to school on time."

I push the backpack up onto my shoulder and wince. None of this is my fault, I want to say. It's on my mom for dying and coming to me this morning like a ghost asking me to see things I shouldn't be seeing. Ms. Park searches me for a moment, looking for what, I don't know, but then she softens and says, "You won't have to take the test again. All I ask is that you get out of bed, no matter how difficult the day, and get to school on time. We can always help you. Small steps, Meg. Incremental steps that will help you see your successes each day. This is what will help you."

I look up from the dingy vinyl floor tiles. I want to tell her the truth, but there is no truth to tell that she doesn't already know. The whole town knows that my mom died and that my dad ran away. They know I live in a garret with Georgia and that I wear my mother's hand-me-downs, some of which were her mother's and her mother's mother's, because I'm too messed up not to. I close my eyes and remember the day Grandad took off his white cotton gloves for the last time. I was twelve years old. I don't know how he knew it was time. Did he know he was going to die? Maybe he had that sixth sense, as Georgia says he did, but it was as if he knew he was going to go. I open my eyes and Ms. Park is staring at me. "My mother died ten years ago today," I explain. "I'm sorry."

"You've been dealt a lot of grief. No one is denying you that, Meg. But we all have grief and we all have pain and we all have..."

"I know," I interrupt.

"You need to go down to the office and get yourself signed in. Go on now. I've made you late. Here," she says, handing me a pink slip of paper. "If you have any trouble getting a pass have them call me." She smiles broadly. "I'm not sorry we've had this chat." You're not sorry, I want to say. Why is no one ever sorry? "Thank you for paying attention in class." She reaches out a wobbly hand and takes ahold of mine. "I appreciate you."

Ceremoniously, like giving a queen her scepter, I remember Grandad handing me a pair of new white gloves and asking me to put them on. "It's time you took this home with you, Meg," he said, placing the last remaining copy of *Fable Island* into my small hands. "Take it and hide it away in a box or put it beside your bed and read it every night. The choice is yours. The book is yours. You..." he said, with tears in his eyes, "are as much a part of this book as your mother was to Fable Island. Never forget that."

I think he hugged me, although I'm not certain I remember it correctly because he wasn't the kind of grandad who hugged. But if he was going to hug me this would have been the day to do it. Maybe I wanted him to hug me. I wanted something, anything that would bring my mom back. I knew she wasn't coming back, but still, I wanted something to make me feel better, and maybe by receiving *Fable Island,* I thought I would.

Ms. Park tightens her grip. "Ten years is a long time to grieve, Meg. A long time." I can't help the tears. "But you're going to be OK. Honest. You just have to give love a chance. You have to remember all the love your mother…"

I pull away from her and stumble toward the door. "Please don't tell me how to feel."

"I am not telling you anything you don't already know, Elida Fay."

I turn to her, surprised. No, stunned. "I hate that name. How did you know it?"

"I have fond memories of your grandad," she says easily. "I used to come into The Book Galley when you were a little girl. I know all about the faeries of Fable Island." I wipe the tears, hastily, on my sleeve. "You're a curious girl, Meg. I've always known that about you. And I've seen that curiosity in my class. It takes a special kind of mind to ask the questions you ask. Curiosity, Meg. That's what drives science." I take another step toward the door. "I taught your mother, you know. A long time ago. Right here in this very room." Ms. Park turns toward the window and smiles. "She, on the other hand, was a daydreamer. Always staring out this window."

I look out over the sea of hastily departed chairs. "Mom was in this room? Looking out this same window?"

"She wore her badge like the invincible warrior she was," says Ms. Park, raising her hand to the ceiling in prayer. "A true queen."

"My mom?"

Ms. Park nods. "Be proud of her, Meg. She served us all well, you know. If it wasn't for your mom we might not have that last remaining copy of *Fable Island*."

"You know...?"

"I know you have the book."

"But how?"

She studies me. "Your grandad told me. And do you know what else he told me? He told me you would be the one to solve the mystery of Fable Island. Is that true? Will you be the one..."

"Oh, my God," I wince, looking at her and laughing painfully. "No one, especially someone who understands science, would ever believe that an imaginary island could be real." At this, Ms. Park grins. "And no one is ever going to find it. OK? It doesn't exist."

"One recognizable success at a time, Meg," she offers. "One and then two..."

I choke on my words as the memories become intense and the tears come fast. "You people are insane! There are no faeries. No Fable Island. And I am not curious. I couldn't care less. No one will ever find the Faerie Queen. Ever."

Six

"The bottom of the ladder is the sturdiest part, Theo," I explain. "We think of the bottom as something bad. Something we should climb up and out of. But if it's the sturdiest, then how can that be bad?" Theo rolls her eyes. "I know I'm at the bottom. But the bottom could be the best part of something. After all, when one climbs up from the bottom one isn't always sure where one will go. This makes the bottom real."

Theo plops down beside me on the sagging twin bed and winces. "You sound so, I don't know, old. Who talks like that?" She grimaces. "It's all those old books you read." I shake my head, but she continues. "So you're admitting you've hit bottom? Then do something about it. How many times have I told you to pick yourself up from the past and get out?"

I answer uneasily, "Too many."

"You need to get out of this creepy attic and move downstairs. Maybe Georgia will let you clean out her art studio. She barely uses it. And then you can take that bedroom for yourself. This one is nothing but a sad reminder of your mom." She picks up one of my worn stuffed animals and tosses it onto the floor. "Her old clothes, her old books, her old furniture. You need your own space. Something more, I don't know, grown up, Meg," she explains.

"I can't."

"You can't or you won't?"

I look at the tall wooden dollhouse collecting dust in the corner of the attic. It was once my grandmother's, or possibly her mother's, and when Georgia moved me up here all those years ago she took the dollhouse out from under the eaves, cleaned it up, threw a fresh coat of white paint over it, and made new cloth dolls for me to play with. "I don't want to move."

"Look at me, Meg. You're stuck. If you're seeing things that aren't there then that's stress. Right? You're hallucinating if you saw Fable Island. It's not real."

I grimace. "I told you everything because I trust you."

"Then trust me. You can't be going around seeing things that aren't there."

I tighten the grip on another one of my stuffed animals, a matted and much-loved puppy, and pull him close to my heart. "I know."

Theo is cautious when she says, "You need sleep. Meds. Something. Maybe my mom can help. She'll talk to you."

"And do what?"

"I don't know. Help?"

"She's got enough on her mind with the baby."

Theo softens. "Look. We've been best friends since kindergarten, Meg. She loves you. And besides, the baby isn't due for another six weeks."

Theo and I have been best friends, more like sisters, ever since kindergarten. It was a difficult time when my mom was sick and I think I clung to Theo. I remember how uncooperative the boys were in Mrs. Crowley's class and how ridiculously the girls acted, running around treating them like they were gods. I just stood by and watched it all play out day after day, completely out of touch with the rules of the game. Theo wasn't interested in chasing boys then, although that's certainly changed. Without siblings of our own, we chose each other and we've been inseparable ever since. But now that she's getting a real sister things might change. I look at her and smile cautiously. I wonder if she thinks becoming a big sister at fifteen is a good idea, but she doesn't seem to be upset about it.

"Are you getting excited?" I chirp.

"Oh my God, I can't wait! I picked out her name. Poppy. Isn't that adorable? I heard it somewhere. Maybe on social. I don't remember. But I had to have it."

"You got to pick out your sister's name? Not your mom or dad?"

"God, no. They wanted Harriet. What a disaster that would be. I told them if they want a cool kid then..." She tosses another one of my favorite stuffed animals, a torn yellow Easter rabbit, into my lap. "Oh, God, sorry. You're cool." I look up at her and she backpedals. "Smart, cool," she offers. "You know what I mean. Cool like that."

"I'm not cool, Theo. It's OK."

"Well, the more you stay holed up in this room depressed and out of touch with reality..."

"I'm not out of touch."

She puts her carefully manicured hands down on my faded blue jeans. "I'm trying to tell you that if you're seeing things then you're starting to lose it. My mom will help you. I'll talk to her."

"No."

"Look, there isn't a single person in this whole town who ever thought Fable Island was real. Except maybe your mom."

"And my dad."

"But no one else. It's an old story, Meg. A tourist thing." She rolls her eyes again and laughs. "It was all those foreigners who came over here thinking it was real. They were the ones who put up the hotels, peddled the book, and cashed in on the fantasy. But they were living in a storybook, Meg. They even built that stupid-looking stone castle. That's our fairy tale. And you still live in it," she says, waving her agitated hand over the dusty nursery.

"Over a hundred years ago people believed in natural wonders, so they believed in faeries. Maybe they were right," I offer.

"They were taken in by hucksters," Theo retorts, using one of her father's favorite words, "who sold Fable Island as someplace exclusive and secretive. But it was a scam. When the fantasy failed to deliver, and no one found the island, businesses tanked. The whole town collapsed."

"But..."

"End of story, Meg," she says, dismissing me. "And besides, Dad has always said that the book was a gimmick, a way to sell a dream to people willing to buy into it. You can't believe in something that's not real."

"I'm not stupid. I know it's not real. But I saw it, Theo," I say frightened. "I saw it rising out of the water. It looked like it's always been there. Like the island belongs."

"Meg, don't," she says, reaching for my tangled hair and smoothing it down like my mom used to do.

"We have thousands of islands off the coast of Maine, and it could have been any one of them, except it wasn't. I know our islands, Theo. I know what direction they lie in and how far off the coast they are. I've studied the charts. This one was different. It was so different..."

"You're hallucinating. My mom will know..."

I push her hand away. "My mom would know what to do."

"I'm sorry, Meg. Let's forget it. I'll believe you if you want me to."

I'm angry. "Don't pity me."

"I don't."

"You're not going to help by pitying me."

"Let's forget it."

"That's worse, Theo," I shout. I pull the puppy to my lips and kiss him on the top of his head. "I will never forget what I saw," I realize, pointing to the open window. "It looked just like the illustrations in the book." Theo frowns. "The fir trees were taller than anything I've ever seen. Taller than what I imagine the California redwoods to be. And they were as emerald green as...as tourmaline."

"OK," she interrupts, hopping off the bed and closing the window abruptly. "I'll go down to the beach with you tomorrow and we'll look for it."

I continue hugging the matted puppy and smile cautiously. "What if we don't see it?"

Theo is practical. "Then we'll come home, eat your birthday lasagna, stuff ourselves with peppermint ice cream, and play Hearts with Georgia like we always do on your birthday."

"Cool," I answer.

"Not cool, Meg, but whatever," she responds, jumping onto the bed and hugging me. "You know I love you and I want to be there for you. Always."

I smile and toss a pink velvet pillow onto the floor. "I want to read you something," I whisper, lifting *Fable Island* from its hiding place and propping it up in my lap. I reach for the white gloves sitting on the bedside table and put them on. "It says here," I continue, pointing to page fourteen, "*Fable Island has the propensity to educate the feeble minds of those whose hearts are too weak to love, too closed to grow, too rambled to trust.*"

Theo complains. "Trust what?"

I look at her like it's obvious. "The faerie lore. Then it says, *The island is inside the hearts and minds of those who believe.*"

Theo picks up the torn bunny. "What does that mean?"

"Then it says," I continue, turning the thin page and running my white-gloved finger over the text and ignoring her, "*When the words, lost in a library of your broken dreams, are found, the way will open.*"

"This is supposed to be a book about faeries. That sounds..."

"I know, right? It sounds like something Georgia would say. Only she doesn't say it quite like this."

Theo complains, "Well, your aunt is into weird shit."

I laugh easily. "Matcha tea is not weird, Theo."

"No, but you know what I mean."

"She's been giving me a hard time about college lately."

Theo pushes escaping white fluff back inside the bunny's ear. "I know. My mom too. I don't know if I want to go," she realizes. "The baby."

"You can't put your life on hold because of their baby."

"No, I know, but I could be helpful. Mom says I need to go to college, but I don't think I have the grades. And the thought of going to school for another four years would make me insane. I don't have it in me." She shakes her head. "I can't do it."

"We can't afford it."

Theo continues to pat the bunny. "You'll find a way. If anyone gets to leave this one-horse town it'll be you. You're smart, Meg. Smart enough not to believe in make-believe," she says, indicating the book.

"I know," I agree, closing *Fable Island* and pulling off the gloves. "But I feel like I'm standing on the precipice of some impending disaster. Like I'm tipping, and my mind and my body will throw me over the edge of a cliff if I don't..."

"God. That sounds scary. If you don't what?"

"That's just it. I don't know."

"People do weird shit when they hear voices, Meg. Are you hearing voices?"

I shake my head. "Not like that. No, it's more like I hear things I know. Or I see things in my mind when I close my eyes. Normal stuff. But still."

"You're not making any sense," she says, grabbing *Fable Island* from me, recrossing her legs, and opening it up to a random page.

"You have to put these on," I instruct, handing her the gloves.

Theo takes the gloves, makes an exaggerated gesture of putting them on like a cartoon doctor about to perform cartoon surgery, and reads, "*Seismic activity and turbulence left the underground caves on Fable Island susceptible to discovery when the ground, pinched and heaved, tore itself loose from some continent in some hemisphere, to drift aimlessly across the sea. The island sits undetected off a rise of coastal land where brightly painted red fishing boats tied to swollen wooden crates bob in gentle waves. On occasion, when a rare blackness descends and the rains stir melancholy, some of the painted skiffs will tear from their moorings to be swept out to sea, perhaps to land unceremoniously on the far shores of Fable Island, but let it be known that this fabled isle rests in a less turbulent atmosphere where storms do not erupt violently. On Fable Island there is something familiar. On any other land, there is loneliness and fear.*" Theo shifts uncomfortably on the bed. "God, what a mouthful."

"Go on," I encourage. "Keep reading."

She takes off the gloves and pushes the book onto me. "You do it. It's too many words."

I lower my voice to a whisper and continue reading. "*The island, called Fable by those who have heard the tales of a place where the faeries live, lies due east of the small boatyard. The first men who arrived on these shores unknowingly looked out upon the island. They set about to cut tall timbers to build a crude log boat but the boat needed a mast to support a cloth so more timbers were cut, and then a fleet of boats was built that would sail upon the waves to distant shores where more forests were cut and more boats were built. These boats required manpower to direct them, but none who sailed past Fable Island knew of its existence, for only the faeries who did not destroy the timbers could see what was. It wasn't until the men saw the faerie light dance upon the waves did they suspect that the fairy tales of their youth might be true. They unfurled their sails and followed the light. The light beckoned, the tales spread, and the search for Fable Island began in earnest."*

"Why are you whispering?" she says annoyed.

I smile. "Because. Listen to this. *Fable Island is a land elusive to some, but not to others. A parcel cut from the indigenous rock (*see illustration I), there are temperate climes known, but the snow-capped mountain range has been left unexplored. Loose granite and exposed jagged rock on the western shore cascade down to the sea in much the same manner as we see on other land masses, yet this land is not like other known lands. Spiraling, cathedral-like firs encompass the island. There are deer trails, no found civilizations, and no known rivers at present, although there is a vast underwater source and cool mountain springs which feed the deciduous island vegetation and contribute to the many species of moss and fungi."*

Theo throws the bunny at me and complains, "You're so weird, Meg. You knew what to look for from the book, so of course you dreamed it up to look this way. This is exactly why Dad says the book is full of bunk."

I reread, "*Fable Island is a land elusive to some, but not to others,*" and close the book uneasily. "I think Mom went. Or maybe she thought she went. I know when she was dying she said she wanted to return."

"Your mom needed hope, Meg. That's what hucksters sell. And this book is a fairy tale of nothing but sweet, sweet hope."

I fold the gloves and put them back on my bedside table, trying my best to ignore the loneliness as it begins to well up inside me again. "I'm glad you can come to my birthday party."

Theo smiles. "I wouldn't miss it. I never have." She leans over the pile of stuffed animals and raggedy cloth dolls to hug me. "I may not always get you, but I do love you. You're more grown up than anyone in our class, probably more grown up than my dad," she says, lifting her eyebrows as if to suggest he was irresponsible for getting her mom pregnant, "and way more grown up than your dad. I'm sorry I told you that you needed to grow up. I love this room," she admits, hopping off the bed and picking up the tossed kangaroo and her joey. "It's so cozy. I wish I hadn't thrown out all my stuffed animals, but it would have been too embarrassing to keep them." She falls back onto the bed, pulls the animals into her lap, and cradles them. "Now I want them all back."

"Here," I offer, handing her my favorite puppy. "Take this one. You can spend the night with it and no one will know you're hugging a lovey." Theo cackles so loudly I'm certain Georgia can hear her downstairs. "Just one more page," I try, pulling on the gloves again and opening *Fable Island* to page seventeen. "I forgot this part. It says, *Long ago when the tales of Fable Island first appeared, there was one who led the way. It was said she beckoned lost sailors and wayward boys with her effervescence..."*

Theo complains. "Gross."

"No. Not like that."

Theo rolls her eyes. "The Faerie Queen isn't real."

I study Theo for a moment and backpedal. "I know. She's a story. Fake. In our imaginations. I get it," I say acquiescing.

Theo hops off the bed and pulls a mottled cardboard box off the shelf. "Remember these?" she says, dumping a set of antique metal train cars onto the floor where they clatter noisily. She takes out several pieces of metal track from another water-stained box and scoots along the floor while laying them down. She looks up at me and smiles. "Remember when we did believe in faeries?" she admits. "When Georgia told us we would see them?" I look away. "She said when we got older they'd find us and we believed her." Annoyed, I close the book. "She didn't want us to grow up," Theo explains, "so, of course, she said that to keep us in the game." I slide down onto the floor beside her and put each of the dented train cars onto the track, making sure that their small worn wheels fit into the metal grooves. Theo puts the final piece of track down on the floor and locks it in place to close the circle. "So, you still read *Fable Island?*" she asks.

"Not really."

Of course, Theo knows I'm lying, but she ignores it. "Want to make a lake?" she offers, jumping up and pulling Mom's wooden boats off the shelf. She puts them down on the floor. "This way we can create a vacation scene."

"What if I do still read it?" I admit, picking at the peeling red paint on one of the tugboats.

Theo lays a piece of blue silk down on the floor and pushes it around until she's satisfied with the shape of her lake. "It's not real."

Our eyes meet, but I don't know what else to say. Instinctively, I look away. "Georgia likes you," I try, putting each of the boats down onto the silk. "She's glad we're friends."

Theo rearranges the boats and then stands up to look down on the scene. "We need a moat," she declares.

"Then we need a castle."

"No, we don't. This is stupid," she admits, abruptly changing her mind. She pulls at the cloth and capsizes the boats.

"Or…"

"Or what?"

"Or some part of you thinks this is fun."

She blushes. "I was bored."

I look at her surrounded by all the toys and smile cautiously. "That's not true."

"You know what I mean. Why are you keeping this shit?" She disassembles the train set and dumps it, piece by dented piece, back into the box. "You should throw it away."

"I can't do that, Theo," I explain, placing the much-loved boats back onto their shelf. "I'd kill my mom all over again if I did."

Annoyed, Theo pushes a loose curl away from her face. "You're drowning in her memory, Meg."

"No. I'm remembering her."

"You're obsessing."

"No…" I try, but the tears are suddenly hard to hide.

Theo puts her hands on her wide hips. "Are you really OK, Meg?"

"I'm OK," I lie.

"Not if you're still reading *Fable Island* and believing…"

"I'm not really reading it. I'm…"

"You're lying, Meg. And friends don't lie to one another. Friends…"

I raise my voice. "Friends support…"

"Friends make sure friends are safe. Are you safe, Meg?" I fold myself down onto the rumpled bed and bury my face into the pillows to hide the tears. "Answer me. Do you feel safe?" But the tears come hard and I can't help but weep. "Shit," she says, hopping onto the bed and pulling me in close. She cradles my head in her lap and strokes my hair. "I'm sorry. God, I'm so sorry, Meg. Forgive me."

Seven

"Of course, I don't believe you saw the island," says Theo, "but I'll read *Fable Island* if you want me to. Because I love you." She slides down onto the floor in her fashionable new jeans, mumbles something again about all the toys in the room, and pulls my worn puppy into her lap. She slips on the gloves and turns the pages of *Fable Island*, but then looks at the closed window and complains, "Geez. It's hot up here." I smile, open the broken window, and wedge an antique metal fire truck, another one of my great-grandmother's toys, between the frame and the window to keep it from closing. I can just make out the kittiwake as she unfurls her gray-tipped wings toward the horizon before aimlessly dipping over the turbulent waves.

While I perch on the window seat and hug my knees to my chest, Theo rereads, *"It was said she beckoned lost sailors and wayward boys with her effervescence—a model of utmost femininity. Although peevish and spoiled, the Faeirie Queen appeared sure-footed and proud."* Theo laughs. "I remember this part from, like, kindergarten when Mom took me to The Book Galley. When your grandad still owned it and would read to us." She studies me for a moment before continuing. *"Call her what you will, but the queen is not like her predecessors, rather she is determined to belong as a faerie belongs to her natural world—one with her surroundings and never apart."* Theo pauses and then lifts the book to show me how heavy it is. "This is a big book with tiny print."

"It's not supposed to be easy to read. It's not a children's book."

Theo runs her finger down the page to find her place again. "What does he mean when he says, *one with her surroundings and never apart?"*

"The Faerie Queen is part of the environment," I answer. "The natural world. She's not separate from nature."

Theo nods and continues. *"Born as a vibrational pattern, the Faerie Queen, not unlike the honeybee, lives to bring the cellular structure of an organism, such as plant material, into herself..."*

"She drinks nectar," I explain.

Theo lifts her eyebrows in uncertainty. *"...so that she can become the structure itself.* Meg, this is ridiculous."

I take the book from her and continue reading. *"She is as much a part of the cellular body of an organism as the organism itself—the stalk, the root, the vibrational essence of life. The queen is an effervescent light being transporting light codes unto herself."*

Theo lies down on the floor and props the puppy up on her chest as if it were hers. "Light codes?"

"Photosynthesis," I answer, watching her tug the fragile puppy's stubby tail.

Theo sits up and shouts, "Then why doesn't he just say that?" I smile, remembering how much I love this book. "I don't know about this, Meg. Isn't *Fable Island* supposed to be about faerie magic? Didn't you tell me it was Neverland?"

"We don't know," I try. "Listen. *She transports herself as light over the plant exchanging codes, a kind of light language naked to the human eye, so that as she brings life-giving light to the organism so, too, does the organism bring her life.*"

"I don't get it."

"She's a way to explain photosynthesis."

"That's it?"

"Well, not entirely. She's a way."

Theo looks bored. "What do you mean?"

"A way of seeing plant life or photosynthesis as vital to all life. Without the Faerie Queen, all life would cease. She is the reason..."

Theo laughs. "She's a character in a book, Meg. Like Tinker Bell."

"Not before she was misconstrued." I turn the page. "It says that long ago in many cultures she was revered as a queen. People came to her temples and worshipped her as the giver of life." I turn to Theo and explain. "Long before contemporary religion."

Theo nods. "Paganism."

"Sort of, but not really," I offer.

Without thinking, Theo kisses my puppy. "Then what was she if she wasn't a pagan queen?"

"Mom once told me, and I think I'm beginning to understand," I explain, watching her twirl my puppy in the air and catch it, "that we all hold the faerie code. Only we've forgotten the magic, and in doing so we've forgotten ourselves."

Theo cradles the puppy and exclaims, "So you're telling me you're a faerie? I'm a faerie! We're all faeries." She laughs. "We're not six years old anymore, Meg."

"Yeah, I know," I concede.

"You're better off sticking with Tinker Bell than trying to explain this book to anyone."

"Yeah, I know, but don't you get it?"

"Yeah, I get it. It's about sex."

"Biology."

"Sex."

"Which is..."

Theo interrupts, "I get it, Meg."

"The faerie lore isn't about a girl. It's about a way of being in tune with our natural world. It's about living in a co-creative relationship with all living things. Faerie lore is about light. About life."

"Is this really what your mom thought?" Theo asks, tossing the puppy aside. "It sounds like a cult."

I frown. "Grandad told me when he gave me the book that I had a choice. I could accept the responsibility I had for myself and the realm. Or not. The choice was mine. But he told me I owed it to my mom to finish..."

"Finish what?"

"Nothing." I turn to look at the ocean tearing itself onto the beach. "We're getting a storm."

"What were you saying about your mom?" Theo asks, ignoring the wind rattling the window panes. "That she died before she...did what?"

"Returned to Fable Island," I answer weakly.

Theo is adamant. "You don't really believe she went. It's impossible."

I close the book. "I don't know anymore."

"You've always said she lied, or your dad lied, or maybe Georgia lied."

"Georgia thinks Mom went to Fable Island when she was sixteen," I respond.

"No way!"

"That's what she said."

"And you believe her?"

"I don't know, Theo," I wail. "Don't you see how messed up this is? I don't know if something's wrong with me or if I'm...normal."

"You're not normal," she says teasing.

"But maybe I am. Maybe I'm more normal than anyone else."

Theo takes the book from me and pulls on the gloves. She impatiently scans the page and reads, "*She alights upon this fair earth with dignity. She is not humble for she knows she has a responsibility to show men, like myself, our propensity to harm. Were it not for the Faerie Queen our desires would go unchecked and our hearts would darken.* What desires?" she asks uneasily.

"The desire to destroy."

"Is that a desire?" Theo asks, sitting next to me on the window bench. A series of rapid-fire freezing rain pellets hit the glass and I turn to close the window. The wind catches it and the window closes with a sharp bang.

I wince. "Some people desire destruction."

Theo grimaces. "How am I ever going to read this whole book? It's so boring."

I take *Fable Island* from her. "You don't have to read it, Theo."

"But I want to."

"It's OK."

"No, it's not. If you need…"

"You know what I need?" I realize, reaching for the gloves. "I need to get out of this room."

"Really?"

"Yeah. My mom haunts me in here."

"I told you. Let's ask your aunt about the studio…"

"No. I need to get out. Leave."

"And go where?"

"I need to find my dad."

Theo raises her voice. "Why?! He's never written to you. Or called. You don't know where he is or if he's even alive."

I catapult myself off the window bench and scoop up the puppy from the floor. "I can't stay here. There's nothing left."

Theo throws herself off the bench and hops from one foot to the other. "You can't just leave!"

"There's no reason to stay."

"Meg, honest to God, this is nuts. You can't run away. You wouldn't know where to go." The sleet continues to assault the peeling frame and we both turn to the window. "I'll only tell Georgia and then you'll just have to come back and do time in this prison cell of yours," she says, waving her hands over the room, "and then what? You'll be right back where you started. You're sad. I get that. And I'm trying to help you, but this mood…well, it gets old, Meg." I stuff *Fable Island*, the white gloves, and the puppy into my backpack. "Meg?!" she shouts.

"You don't understand, Theo. I can't help the way I feel."

"No, I know, but I think my mom…"

"I want my own mom," I wail.

"But you have her," Theo explains, waving her hands around the room at my mother's clothes, her furniture, and her books.

"I don't have her, Theo. I have fragments of her. It's not enough."

"But at least it's something. My mom…"

"Will you stop talking about your mom? We're talking about my mom."

"I know, but…"

I turn from her and stuff a pair of mismatched socks, underwear, a hairbrush, and an oversized down vest into the backpack. "I don't want to talk about it."

"Meg. You can't just go. You're getting weird. I don't understand. I'm your best friend. You can't just leave."

"Maybe I can't be your friend. Maybe I…" I cry, fumbling with the zipper on my backpack.

Theo pulls me into her. "Shh…your aunt will hear you. Do you want her to come up here? Come on. Sit down for a minute and let's figure this out."

"I don't want this 'everyone is happy' shit."

"I never said everyone was happy."

Georgia knocks quickly before opening the door. "Everything all right with you two?"

"No," answers Theo easily.

Georgia studies the backpack and frowns. "Going somewhere, Meg?" she asks.

"To Theo's," I lie.

"No, she's not," Theo answers. "She…"

"Come on girls. That's enough bickering. Your father called, Meg. I came up here to tell you." She says it as easily as if my father calls all the time. As if it was normal. "I told him that we'd call him back if that was all right with you."

"We?" I wince.

Theo dances onto the tips of her toes. "He called?!" she asks in disbelief.

"I don't believe you," I shudder, tightening the grip on the backpack and pushing past my aunt.

"I didn't believe it at first," Georgia answers, taking ahold of my arm. "I almost didn't answer the phone. But then I recognized the number. He's not here, Meg, but he is alive. And," she says hesitating, "he remembered your birthday. He called to…"

"To do what?" I shout. "Apologize?"

"Maybe that's good," Theo tries.

Georgia is abrupt. "He called to ask if you've seen the bridge to Fable Island, Meg." She looks down at my overstuffed pack with its contents spilling out. "And to encourage you to go."

"You're lying," I hiss.

"No, I am not lying." She takes the backpack from me and steers me back into the room. "You're not going to like this, but I'll tell you the rest. Sit down," she says, tilting her head toward the rumpled bed. Theo pulls me down next to her, wide-eyed and expectant, and grabs ahold of my hand. Georgia pauses. She looks around the room until her eyes land on the trunk of my great-great-grandmother's old clothes.

"Are you just going to stand there and let me guess?" I shout.

"No. I'm going to sit down next to you," she says, dropping the backpack to the floor and taking my other hand in hers, "and tell you that your father is not well." She looks at the copy of *Fable Island* sticking out of the pack, "He says that you are to go. For him. For us. For all of us."

I pull away from them both and stand. "He's an asshole."

Georgia takes a deep breath, and when she lets it out slowly she answers, "I told you I didn't know where he was or if he was even alive. And that was the truth, Meg," she says, standing and taking me in her arms. "But now we know he's alive. I just don't know for how long."

"Where is he?" I shout.

Looking over at Theo, Georgia gives her that tilt of her head toward the door that says, "please go," but Theo ignores her and curls up on my bed and pulls the stuffed animals into her lap. "Thailand."

"Thailand!" I shriek.

"I don't know the extent of things, but he's not well. He said..."

"How did he get to Thailand?"

"He's married, Meg."

"Shit," says Theo under her breath.

"And he seems to think that's OK?" I cry. "That's not OK."

"No," says Georgia easily. "I will agree with you there. That's something he should have told us."

"Why you, Georgia?" I hiss. "He should have told me!"

"Because we're in this together, Meg," she responds. She turns to Theo. "Do me a favor, love, and call your mom to come pick you up. I'm not sure this is the best night for you to be here."

Georgia called Theo "love" and I pull away from them both in disgust. "I'm staying," says Theo. "I'm going to be here when

Meg turns sixteen. When the clock strikes midnight I will be with her. She needs me."

I can't believe what I'm hearing. "No one thinks that because I'm turning sixteen I will see a bridge. You're out of your mind. All of you," I say frightened.

Georgia reaches down to the floor and pulls *Fable Island* out of the pack. "This is the last surviving copy of the most famous book the world once knew, Meg. Right here. In my hands. I won't let you lose sight of that. And if you don't see a bridge and you never go to Fable Island so be it," she declares, "but if you don't at least try…"

I turn from her and fling myself onto the bed. "I can't."

"Meg saw the island this morning," Theo admits.

Georgia exclaims, "Is that true?! This morning?"

Theo looks toward the window and raises an eyebrow. "She told me she saw it rising out of the water. Out there."

Georgia smiles. "Is that what you were doing down there this morning?"

Theo strokes my hair. "She might be OK. I don't know."

"I'm fine," I shout, pushing her away.

Georgia pulls the book to her chest and looks at Theo. "For certain?" she asks.

"I'm fine," I try again. "And yes, I did see it."

"What about the bridge?" she asks excitedly. "Do you think…?"

I turn to Theo. "Do you see why I'm so messed up? My dad left and now he wants me to save him. Son of a bitch."

"Your father is the one who messed things up," Georgia admits. "I think if he could have stayed he would know what to do…"

I hiss, "But he didn't!"

Georgia is curt. "No."

"He left me."

"He left us," she tries.

Theo trills nervously, "You're going to be OK, Meg."

I turn to Georgia. "Are you telling me the truth?"

She puts her hand to her heart. "He said he was in Thailand. I have no reason to doubt him."

"And my mom? Where is she?" I cry.

Georgia closes her eyes, and with her long slender hand still on her heart, she sits down next to me on the bed and whispers, "Gone."

"How come you never cry about her?" I wail. "And how come you're so mean to me about all of this?"

Georgia answers easily, "You and I are two very different people, Meg. I don't know if what I am is practical, and you take that for meanness, but if you're telling me the truth about the island then I have every reason to believe you'll see the bridge." She smiles. "I'm not so practical that I don't believe in magic."

"But why me?" I wince.

"Why not you?"

"But why not you? Or anyone else?"

Georgia says, "Your father could answer that one, Meg."

"Well...will he?" I cry.

"I don't know."

"You should call him," Theo suggests. "Call him and ask him."

Eight

Sometime in the middle of the night, I awake to the sound of the rain hitting the side of the house. Had it not been for Theo curled up beside me, I probably wouldn't have fallen asleep. But when we texted her mom and asked her what I should do about calling my dad, her mom told me it would be a good idea. "Maybe he can tell you more about your mom," she suggested. A practical idea, I reasoned. Perhaps I did need Theo's mom after all.

Now deep in sleep, Theo breathes heavily beside me as the wind rattles the rotting window panes. Georgia says she can't afford to replace the windows or repair the sills. "Artists don't make enough to live in today's world," she often tells me. "And the taxes on this place are through the roof. I will deplete my inheritance before you're gone, but I will never move you. Not from our family home."

My sense of time is distorted. There is a hazy pink light illuminating the horizon where the sky and the ocean meet, but it feels too early to be dawn. I reach for Gramma's gold watch, but the hands are too small to read in the dim light and my phone is dead. I must have forgotten to plug it in. At the stroke of midnight, when we were both wide awake, Theo and I ran to the window and stared at the churning ocean, but the dark and the rain and the veiled windows made it impossible to see anything. I laughed painfully at the thought of a bridge that would take me to Fable Island, and through my angry tears, I told Theo more of my father's lies.

I can tell by the way the rain hits the floor that the window has been left open. I scramble out of bed and peer out at the dark ocean. "Theo," I whisper uneasily, "you left the window open." Just enough light is coming into the room from under the bedroom door to see that the floor is getting soaked. Georgia must have left a lamp on downstairs because the light spills out onto the steep rocky lawn, creating distorted shadows. Quickly, I close the window, tiptoe over the wet floorboards, grab a quilt from the bed, and throw it down onto the floor. I take off my T-shirt and socks and toss them aside. Rummaging in the closet for something dry to put on, I settle on a plaid flannel shirt, and hastily button it up. Theo stirs and I hear her gentle wheezing, but when she turns over in her sleep and settles onto her side, she quiets.

I slip back into bed, but I can tell something isn't right. It's not my mother. At least it doesn't feel like her. Sometimes when I feel her presence, it feels like a weight on my chest and there are words or ideas that need to come out of me and be spoken aloud, but this is not one of those times. Rather, it feels more like some strangeness has descended upon the room. I reach for the lamp and turn on the yellow bulb. It illuminates the torn paper shade and casts an eerie glow. Theo stirs again. "Theo," I whisper, scanning the room. Nothing looks out of place, everything is where it belongs, but I hop out of bed and close the lid to the trunk, which holds my great-great-grandmother's Edwardian lace gowns and silk petticoats. Some of them have spilled out and look creepy, as if some part of her buried past will come back to life.

Before my mother got sick she encouraged dress-up play. Together we would put on the scratchy gowns and hold tiny knitting needles, the size of toothpicks, to knit warm scarves for the Faerie Queen. We were certain that if we didn't, she would get cold. Mom would smile and remind me how kindness toward the faeries went a long way. She would tell me that we wouldn't have so much anger in the world if everyone was kind. My father would scoop her up in his arms, lift her off the rocky ground, and remind her that there would always be anger in a world as violent as ours. But my mother insisted that if we were kind to the faerie realm then kindness would follow us all of our days.

At low tide, when most of the beach stones were no longer covered by the shifting ocean waves, we would put the miniature scarves, acorns, flower petals, seaweed nests, and trinkets that were vital to the queen down on one of the granite rocks. The next day when we skipped down to the water's edge, and the gifts had been received, my mom was happy. We had been kind to the faeries and in doing so they, in turn, would be kind to us. I didn't want to believe that the waves had taken our treasures out with the tide. But I knew.

My great-great-grandmother's large-brimmed hats had long ago lost their brightly-colored feathers, and the lace had been torn from the gowns, but Mom always encouraged theatrics, and when she was feeling well she wrote stage plays. They were sentimental plays about "the real" (her words) Peter Pan and Wendy. Mom believed that if she wrote the true story of Fable Island and not the made-up crocodile version, then everyone would realize that the Faerie Queen was real and not some haughty princess. Looking back on it, Mom was always writing these plays.

I remember dressing up in her trailing gowns and tripping over the ragged hems as I tried to walk. I always played the part of Wendy, and my mother, Peter, although her stories didn't have swords, one-armed captains, or Lost Boys. These stories were about the guardianship of the faerie realm. And it was Peter who taught Wendy to protect the faeries and give them a proper home on the island where they would never be exploited or ruined.

"Theo," I whisper again, and she stirs.

"What?" she says groggily.

"Never mind. Sorry to wake you."

"Are you OK?" she mutters.

"Yeah, you left the window open. Rain was coming in everywhere."

Theo sits up. "I didn't open the window."

"You must have opened it before we went to bed."

She hesitates. "No, I didn't."

"Well, that's weird," I complain. "Are you sure?"

She looks toward the window. "Yeah. It's raining. I wouldn't..."

"I guess it opened itself then."

"Meg!" she sputters.

"It's nothing. I must have done it."

Theo rolls out of bed. "The floor is wet."

"Yeah. We'll deal with it in the morning."

"Are you sure we shouldn't..."

I turn out the light. "No, it's OK. Sorry to wake you."

Theo crawls back into bed. "Did you see how much water there is? Maybe we should tell Georgia."

"No, she'll just get mad. I'll take care of it in the morning. Go back to sleep."

"Is the room rocking?" she asks sleepily.

"It's the wind."

Theo rolls over onto her side, and before I can fall asleep again, her breath slowly returns to its usual rhythmic pattern. I listen to the wind assaulting the side of the house. It sounds like one of those violent nor'easters, where we will discover many lost roof shingles, broken branches, and downed trees in the morning.

Without warning, something is knocked off my dresser and it lands with a dull thud on the floor. "Who's there?" I stammer, bolting upright in bed. Theo mumbles something. "Hello?" I shudder. Except for Theo's occasional exhaling "pift," nothing seems out of place. I turn on the light. "Is anyone there?"

Theo stirs. "Who are you talking to?"

"No one," I realize. "There's no one. I just thought I heard..."

"Your room is haunted."

"Don't say that," I try, looking uneasily at the black metal Rolls Royce, one of Gramma's old toys, that has been knocked to the floor. The car is battered from years of play. I'm sure that after my great-grandmother was through with it she gave it to Gramma who gave it to my mom and Georgia, who, in turn, gave it to me. "It's me. I can't get over the fact that I was thinking about running away. I was so sure I'd be able to find my dad."

Theo is blunt. "That would have been impossible."

"But then, like magic, he called."

Theo hugs my puppy. "I know. That was so weird."

"What do you think it means?"

"It's spooky." She pulls the stuffed animals protectively around us. "So what did your aunt mean when she said you owned the last copy of *Fable Island*? That's the only one? And why does your dad know something about you that no one else knows? Can you talk about it now?"

"No," I answer. "I don't know and I don't care."

"But what if," she tries, "he's dying? He said he needs your help."

"I don't trust him, Theo. He can't suddenly come back into my life and expect me..."

"But you wanted him."

"No, not really. I wanted something, but I'm not sure it was my dad I wanted to find."

Theo shudders. "Did you hear that?"

I look down at the Rolls Royce now tipped on its side. "No."

She pulls me into her. "Who's there?" she whispers.

"No one."

"What if someone is under the bed?"

"They wouldn't fit."

"Why? More toys?"

"School projects."

"Check the closet," she begs. "I know I heard something."

"It was the wind," I say to reassure her. "It always does this when it storms."

"You've got me creeped out."

I laugh. "It feels like we're on a boat. The floor is tipping. Everything is sliding one way and then..."

Theo panics. "No, it doesn't. Come on. Quit it."

"And water is sloshing over the sides," I add. "Things are falling."

Theo pulls the blankets up to her chin. "Turn on all the lights, Meg. You're freaking me out."

I laugh. "I'm kidding."

"Then stop it."

"Come on, let's get some sleep," I manage, turning out the light. But somehow I know the Rolls Royce didn't just spontaneously roll itself off the dresser. It's been stuck in the same spot for years.

Theo curls her warm body next to mine and wraps her plump arms around my waist. "This house is weird."

I grimace. "I know."

She is quiet for a while before she whispers, "So is the book valuable? If it's the only one?"

"No. No one reads it anymore."

"Maybe it should be in a museum? Or a library?"

"Yeah, probably. They would put it under glass and protect it."

"You could donate it," says Theo thoughtfully.

"Yeah. But I won't. I need it."

Before long, Theo is asleep, and her arm around my waist slackens. I slip out of bed, careful not to wake her, pick up the antique car, and put it back on the dresser where I've kept it all these years. Although I no longer play with the toys in the room, they are a reminder of a playful childhood, one that if I could put the pieces back together again, I would. "I don't know what you want from me, Mom," I whisper, "but quit it. I mean it."

Half expecting her to open the door and glide into the room in one of her floor-length gowns, but knowing full well that she never will, I open the door and peer down the attic steps. The light is spilling out into the hallway from inside Georgia's bedroom and illuminating the uneven floorboards. Closing the attic door behind me, I tiptoe down the stairs careful not to slip, and knock on her open door. "I can't sleep," I explain.

Georgia takes off her reading glasses, puts down her book of essays, and grimaces."Neither can I," she says, patting the bed next to her and inviting me in. "I take it you've been watching for the island." I stand in the doorway, unsure how to answer her. She turns toward the windows where the rain continues to pummel the house. "I've been watching for it all night, but it's black as pitch out there." I want to tell her to turn out the light and go to sleep. "I'm sure there will be more shingles blown off and more mess in the yard. We'll probably lose another one of your great-grandmother's maples. They've been on their way out for years."

I lean on the newly repainted door frame. Georgia insists we keep all the trim in the house high-gloss white, and the walls celadon, just like her grandmother did. "Why didn't you clean out this place after Grandad died? And why do you keep everything…"

"The same?" she answers, lifting herself out of bed. She runs her tired eyes down my flannel shirt and then to my cold bare legs. "Are you OK? Do you want a cup of tea?"

"No. I was just wondering why we can't move forward."

She frowns. "What do you mean?"

Like the rest of the house, the room is drafty, and her crisp lace curtains ripple with each gust of wind. Georgia takes my hand, pulls me into the room, and closes the door. "I wasn't expecting this storm." Together we sit down on her stiff bed. It is covered in colorful old quilts, but unlike my bed, they are uniformly stacked, and all the corners of the quilts fall precisely the same way, evenly, down the sides. For an artist, Georgia is unusually meticulous. "Are you sure you don't need anything?" The wind rocks the house and she tightens her grip. "Mercy," she shrieks, "are we going to lose the house?" She stiffens. "Where's Theo?"

I nod, indicating my room upstairs. "Asleep."

"In this?"

"Yeah, I know."

She pulls me into her and hugs me. It's the first time I think I genuinely feel her take the time to hug me properly, and I soften. "Happy birthday, Megan Elida Fay," she whispers. I let her hold me, briefly, before pulling away. She looks up at the ceiling and grins. "You might need to wait upstairs in the nursery."

I frown. "Why did Dad really call?"

"I don't know. I assume he wants to make things right before he leaves this world and transitions to another."

I watch the curtains. "What do you mean? He's dying?"

"He didn't say, but…" She quiets. "He gave me the impression that things weren't good. That maybe he wasn't ready to go. He wanted you to, I don't know, help pause his death by going to the island."

I'm getting mad and I hiss, "I can't do that. And neither could he."

She lets her eyes follow mine until they, too, land on the shifting curtains. "You can either ignore the request to call him back or call."

"He doesn't deserve anything from me."

"Choose one," she offers. "Call or don't call. You won't be making a wrong decision either way."

"I don't think I can."

"No. I imagine you've had enough hurt."

"But what does he want?"

"He wants to leave this world with his dignity still intact," she answers stiffly. "Otherwise, you will haunt him."

"No, I won't."

She takes hold of my hand again. "I'm convinced we're haunted by those who need to put things right."

"What do you mean?"

"Just that," she says, turning anxiously toward the windows as the rain picks up in intensity. "Sometimes I think my father is here with me, but I don't ever see him. Maybe I feel his presence…" she admits, but her voice trails off.

Without warning Theo throws the door open and takes a running leap onto my great-grandmother's four-poster bed. "There's a…a…there's someone in your room, Meg!" she cries.

Georgia looks up at the ceiling. "I knew it," she whistles. "Go! You need to go upstairs, Meg."

"Who is it?" I shout, pulling Theo into me.

Panicked, Theo wails, "I swear to God..."

"No," says Georgia cautiously. "Don't swear. He's harmless." She looks up at the ceiling again and smiles. "Promise me, girls, you'll trust me on this."

"I knew something wasn't right. I felt it."

"Do you think you will ever trust me, Meg?" Georgia asks, shaking me playfully as if to knock some sense into me.

Theo is scared. "What's going on? Who is it?"

"Trust me," she whispers, looking again at the ceiling. "Don't be frightened."

"But I saw someone!"

"I understand, Theo, but let me explain."

"He must have come in through the window," I realize.

Georgia is excited. "Precisely! That's how it's supposed to happen. At least that's what your mom told us."

Theo's eyes widen. "Told you what, Georgia?"

"Go!" she says, urging me off the bed. "He's waiting."

Theo looks like she's about to be sick. "I saw him, Meg. I know I saw him."

Georgia pulls Theo into her arms. "This is what we've been waiting for." She looks at me and smiles. "For sixteen years."

Theo is adamant. "Something's not right."

"Listen, Theo. This is an important night. Megan's a pivotal person in our family..."

"You're always saying that, Georgia."

"But it's true," she responds. "Meg's great-great-grandad, the ship's captain who built this house, was a pivotal person too. He knew about the magic," she whispers.

"Don't," I say, warning her.

"Go," she pleads. "You don't want to lose this chance..."

Theo is worried. "Go where?"

"It's unprecedented, really, that in these modern times, you would get this opportunity, Meg. Please go for your father. Can you do this? Just this one time. If not for him then for your mother."

Theo holds onto Georgia and cries, "Where is she going?"

"Where she belongs."

"Stop it!" I shout. "I'm not going. I never said I believed you. Or my mom." I turn to Theo. "Did you invite some guy over?"

"Oh my God, no!"

"Then you were dreaming," I wince.

"I wasn't dreaming," she shouts. "He crowed like a freaking rooster and woke me up!"

"That's him!" says Georgia confidently.

"He looks like Peter Pan!"

"Go, Meg! Just go see what he wants."

"No! You go..."

"Maybe I should go," says Theo.

"No," says Georgia holding her. "This isn't yours."

"But I was the one who saw..."

Georgia pushes me toward the door. "Go! He's waiting, Meg. I think this is how your mother went to Fable Island...how Mr. Barrie, who was invited to stay upstairs in that very room," she says explaining, "hoped to see him. You see, Theo, Meg's great-great-grandfather met him on one of his ocean voyages and he invited Mr. Barrie, the author, to stay here and…"

Theo interrupts, "For real your mom saw Peter Pan?"

Georgia is serious. "That's what she told us. And I've always believed her. But we think Sir Barrie," she says, correcting herself, "couldn't find the island as Meg's great-great-grandad promised him he would, so he went back to England and wrote a completely different story. A different fairy tale. You know the one." As an aside, she adds, "Filled with his insecurities. His frailties."

"Who wrote what?" asks Theo, looking nervously at the ceiling.

Georgia says, "Peter won't hurt you, Meg. He's come to escort you over the bridge." I throw Georgia this look that says, "Please stop talking now," but she continues.

"Theo, from what we understand, Meg's great-great-grandad gave Sir Barrie a night in the attic in exchange for the rights to his soon-to-be-produced stage play. I'm certain he wanted to capitalize on Prof. Yardley's book or he wouldn't have offered Sir Barrie the room. They both wanted the story. And her great-great-grandad knew that if he could prove the island existed, as Prof. Yardley once promised, then he would get rich. Well, they both would. And so Sir Barrie promised to write it true, just as he experienced it. But we think the faeries failed him. He went back home to England and wrote his own story which had nothing to do with the real magic of Fable Island."

I look up at the ceiling half expecting the water to start dripping through the attic floorboards and down onto Georgia's bed. "He took the idea and wrote his own Peter," she continues.

"But he wrote it all wrong, Theo. He made it up. She turns toward me and waves her hands toward the door urging me to go. "But Meg is tasked, as her mother was tasked, as her mother was tasked, as her mother was tasked, and as her mother was tasked," she says exhaling theatrically, "with putting it right."

Theo is incredulous. "Fable Island is real?"

"Meg, darling," says Georgia. "There are no mermaids on Fable Island, but there is, perhaps, wonder. And that, my dear girl, is why your father called. It's time you rewrite *Peter Pan.*"

Nine

The house continues its uneasy rocking as if in one swift motion it will be pulled from its crumbling foundation and tumble down the rock face. "You're lying, Georgia," I wince.

"Don't doubt the magic, Meg," she responds.

"Maybe we can both go," Theo suggests.

Georgia looks at Theo and emphatically shakes her head, no. "This is for Meg."

"Prove it," I bristle.

"When your mother and I lived in this house together as children, she insisted on staying in the attic so your grandad moved a cot up there for her. She believed in the magic," she says, tightening her flannel robe. "I certainly didn't understand it then, nor was I ever invited to stay up there, but I respected the story. This was for her." She studies Theo for a moment before turning to me. "As this is for you, Meg."

I throw my hands up in the air. "Then how do you know what you're talking about? You never went to the island."

Quickly, she rummages under her bed for a pair of slippers and puts them on. "No. I did not. I didn't know how to get there. But when I found my mother's diaries much later, they helped me figure it out. So that's why I put you up in the attic, Meg. So you could..."

I can't help but cringe. "You put me up there? More like banished..."

"I wanted you to grow up with the magic," she explains.

"Faerie magic?" asks Theo.

Georgia is quiet. "My father didn't exactly encourage us to believe in Fable Island." She turns away, pained. "He didn't discourage it. We talked about it, and obviously, he valued the book, but Gramma was quiet and didn't know how to share her experience so my father, well, he took her enthusiasm for it and..."

"Grandad was honest," I say, defending him.

"He was always nice," Theo adds.

Georgia nods uneasily. "But you, Meg," she says, "I wanted you to approach this day, your sixteenth birthday, with an understanding. You're one of the very few who will have this opportunity to go to the island. Too many children outgrow their hope."

Theo is blunt. "I was the one who saw him so maybe I should go."

I turn to Theo and shout, "How can you believe her?!"

"I don't know! Maybe I do!" She shares a look with Georgia. "Do you think I saw Peter Pan? He had wings," she says, wrinkling her nose. "Peter Pan isn't supposed to have wings."

I can't help but scream. "Wings?"

"You need to go upstairs, Meg," Georgia tries, taking me by the hand and pulling me toward the door. We both turn toward the windows as another band of hard-driving sleet pelts the glass. "Come on, Meg. This is the chance of a lifetime. If you go upstairs…"

"Why me?!"

"Because you're the reason he's here! It's your sixteenth birthday, Meg. Go! Go! It has to be Peter," she exclaims. "He's here to help you over the bridge."

Theo suddenly seems mad and she turns toward the door. "I need to go home. Your house is haunted."

Georgia spins me around in a waltz turn. "It's Peter Pan!"

"Never mind. I'm calling my mom."

I pull away, annoyed, and turn toward Theo. "There's no one up there. Don't call your mom."

Theo is suddenly furious. "Is this some kind of joke, Georgia?"

Impatiently, Georgia throws her hands into the air. "No! This isn't a joke, Theo. Meg's dad did call this afternoon. Which I wasn't expecting. But I was expecting magic tonight. Or at least I was hoping for magic. For Meg. She's been through a lot, Theo."

Theo is curt. "We've all been through a lot, Georgia."

"Yes. You've been through a lot with your mom and dad," she offers. "Divorce is painful. It's a loss no one, who hasn't gone through it, understands. But I understand. I do. When my sister died, Meg's father drank himself under the table for three consecutive days and then disappeared. Her grandad and I were unexpectedly tasked with taking care of a six-year-old child, and well, my husband refused to join us here." She is quiet for a moment then turns toward the windows. "Where else were we going to go, Meg? I had to bring you home where I knew you needed to grow up. Where your mother and I grew up. Where her mother, and her mother, and her mother before her grew up." She turns to me. "I'm just grateful my father took us in."

I look away, ashamed. "I didn't know I was the reason for your divorce."

"Well, I don't talk about it. It wasn't your fault. But I do know what Theo is going through is painful." She turns to Theo and smiles stiffly. "But now that your dad is back…"

"He's not back. Not like he should be. He's not going to be living with us."

"Well, your parents are figuring out what works best for them so that's a good thing."

"They're not figuring out what's best for me."

"It's their dilemma."

Theo snaps, "And mine."

"Shh…" I whisper. "I hear him. He's coming down the stairs. Shit. Why is he walking? Isn't he supposed to fly?"

Theo leaps onto her toes. "I want…"

Georgia pushes me toward the door. "Go, Meg. This is yours." She pulls Theo out of the way. "I don't want Peter to see us."

"But I was the one…"

"I'll go," I answer quietly. "Stay here."

Georgia pulls Theo back from the door. "This is for Meg."

"Hello!" I call, taking a step into the dark hallway. "Are you there?" No answer. "Hello?" Again, no answer. I turn back around, but Georgia closes the door so hard it rattles the frame. "What do I do now?" I whisper. No answer. I take another step. "Peter?" I try. "Anyone?" But there is only the sound of the wind and the occasional groan and snap of a falling tree branch. I hold my breath and let it out slowly. "Mom?"

Deliberately, I climb the attic steps and pray this is not something I will come to regret.

Ten

Any number of things that could have happened the morning of my sixteenth birthday, didn't happen. Or I should say, everything that was supposed to happen didn't. The storm marched headfirst along the coast and then circled back on itself, assaulting everything in its way. It moved out sometime in the early hours, making way for a cleansing wind to push it farther up the coast and out to sea. And just as the stars slipped momentarily into view from behind their clouded veil, the sun rose over the horizon shifting the sleepless night into day. Although it was my sixteenth birthday, the one day out of all the possible days of my life when I was supposed to become someone special and experience faerie magic, Earth did not tilt in my favor to make that happen.

I toss another log into my great-great-grandad's oversized stone fireplace. Just as we have done every Christmas Eve since Georgia and I have lived together, we have made a fire and stared into the smoldering embers. Earlier in the afternoon, before sundown, I slipped on my down vest and my new winter boots (an early present), and with the long laces untied, pushed my way through newly fallen snow to collect the logs. Georgia chose not to hire someone to cut down the maple, which had become irrevocably damaged during the nor'easter. She did it herself using a small chainsaw and Grandad's axe.

The log falls off the smoldering stack, lands on the cracked slate hearth, and rolls. "Shit," I complain. Our wood is too green to burn properly and this is why the fire smolders. I reach for a pair of heavy iron tongs, pick up the fallen log, and carefully put it back in place. Georgia says that three logs will burn better than two because they create better airflow. Three has always been better than two, I think. Being in a family of two was never my choice.

Since that night, when all that could have gone wrong, did, Georgia and I can't talk to one another without fighting. It's not the end of the world. It could be worse. When she demanded last summer that I help with the fallen tree, and I fought her on it, she gave me an ultimatum. Either I come downstairs and become a part of our family or she would force me to go to therapy. After all these years alone with my thoughts, and no desire to share them with a stranger, I put on a pair of Gramma's work gloves and went outside to help. I spent a lot of long afternoons cleaning up the mess, but I did it. Uniformly stacked, the newly cut logs have made something about my uncertain life feel more certain.

I'd rather we had dry seasoned wood to burn, but green is all we have. I could quit trying to coerce the fire, as it is rather annoying after four attempts to watch it repeatedly fail to catch. I'm often reminded of failure. It pushes up against me time and time again. Not once has Georgia said she was sorry about that night, nor has she acknowledged the possibility of someone other than Peter Pan entering the house through the attic window. But because I never saw what Theo saw, and that has made me a failure on multiple accounts, Georgia has quietly curbed her enthusiasm for the faerie realm once and for all.

Theo, on the other hand, has made it very clear that she will never set foot in our house again. We don't talk much anymore. After Georgia coaxed Theo out of the dark closet where my aunt forced her to go, I swore to Theo over my mother's dead body, as she promised me I would have to do, that I did not see Peter Pan, or anyone for that matter, when I went back upstairs to the nursery. Consequently, Theo fell into a kind of displaced anger toward me. I don't think she became angry with me because I didn't see him, but rather she became angry because I didn't corroborate her story, which made it appear to her that I wasn't her friend.

I guess you could say we continue to ignore the whole night. All of us. Maybe I've pushed it down and hidden it so when I'm reminded of Peter Pan, or some strange sequence of storm-related phenomena that occurred, it doesn't bother me anymore. I won't lie. It did at first. Shouldn't I have been the one to see him? It made no sense that Theo saw the one thing I was supposed to see, and although I believed her, at the same time part of me didn't. So we live in that unspoken place where what she saw was impossible to believe but at the same time possible. Because it happened to Theo, who never would have made it up, I should have believed her because that's what friends do. But I didn't.

I miss her. I feel within every fiber of my being that she will knock on our door and return just as friendly and fun as she's always been. But as the days slip by and she comes to school less and less, I'm beginning to worry we may never repair this divide. I know she struggles. Her mom went into early labor not too long after that night and lost the baby. It was a rare complication due to her mother's age, the obstetrician said, but Theo wasn't thinking about her mother's age or the probability of something going wrong. She wanted that baby. I'm sure she thinks about how close her mom came to dying and she grieves, not only for her baby sister but for the unimaginable. Yet here I am, a reminder of what can happen. The imaginable.

I grieve for us. I think we could still be friends because we both have heartbreak in common, but she doesn't want to be reminded of that night, or the baby, or the fact that her mom and dad are now estranged. I am a reminder of what went down on a night that was supposed to be fun. Instead, it became the defining moment that pushed us apart. We're not the same people we used to be because of one supernatural event. I haven't seen the island again if I ever did see it. I don't know now that I did. Didn't I? I often think about how desperate I must have been, my mind wounded and needing some kind of hope, so I can only imagine that what I saw was a strange mirage.

I go to school on time, but Theo is often absent. I know she's lost the drive to finish, but I wish she wouldn't deliberately fail. Why? I guess she feels a short-term desire to be happy, so she stays home to be happy in the moment, which we're told is OK, but then again, what's going to happen if no one plans for the future? Georgia never has to wake me up or force me out of bed in the mornings and I'm proud of that. I feel older and more capable. I don't need fairy-tale stories or my childhood room to remind me of all that I have lost. Georgia, without hesitating, cleaned out her studio when I asked her if I could move my bed downstairs. Nothing more needed to be said. Maybe she was sad about losing the attic nursery and all the contents of her past, first to her sister and then to me, but she was also glad I asked her for the grown-up room.

We packed the toys into cardboard boxes and stuffed them under the eaves, sorry to do it, but not sorry at the same time. The choices we made after that night define us today. I am sixteen years old and studying harder than ever to remove myself from a life that I feel deliberately pushes us forward and out of the past.

I stop momentarily and stare into the smoldering fire. "But at what cost, Peter? Why should we grow up?"

"Who are you talking to?" asks Georgia, slipping quietly into the room with a tray of homemade cakes.

I drop the iron tongs on the hearth. "Nobody."

She places a red metal tray adorned with Swedish flower cut-outs on the coffee table, a converted wooden lobster trap that washed ashore a couple of decades ago. Weathered and splintered in places from its earlier life in rough waters, the trap does a nice job as a table. Grandad sanded the jagged edges and placed a large piece of oval glass over the top of it. When the metal tray hits the glass, the glass pings. "Should we call your father?" she asks.

I stuff a large wad of newspaper under the teepee of logs, hoping that the whole mess will catch fire. "Probably."

Ever since that night, when I didn't see Peter Pan and such a huge part of me felt like a failure, I realized I still needed my dad. I call him occasionally. We don't talk about much. We dance around the truth. I ask how he is. He asks how I am. He says that he misses me and I tell him that I will never sell the last remaining copy of *Fable Island.* Do I really believe that I will find the island? No. But sometimes it's easier to lie than tell the truth, just as it's sometimes easier to ignore the truth than accept it.

"Do you think Dad will ever come home," I ask, "and get medical care?"

Georgia hands me one of her grandmother's white linen napkins and a slice of cardamom cake on a decorative china plate. "No. He refuses proper care," she says annoyed. "Without it, I'm sure he's in a lot of pain."

"But then why doesn't he go to a doctor?"

"He should," she says, slicing a piece of cake for herself. "Otherwise the cirrhosis will become unbearable."

"He's not so broken that he wouldn't get help, is he?" This is Georgia's word for my dad. My grandad's word. "Broken."

"Your father moves to the beat of his own drum, Meg," she says. These, too, were Grandad's words. I once heard him say, in anger, unkind things about my dad. "Drunkard. Irresponsible. Flagrant." Georgia is simply repeating words her father once used.

"He's never very forthcoming about anything with me," I admit. "Why doesn't he want to see me?"

She lifts a forkful of cake. "Your father has refused to accept responsibility for you. Period. End of story. And because he has refused, he has cut himself off. And because he has cut himself off, he doesn't know you. Consequently, he has no idea who you are, what your interests are, or about your propensity for seriousness." She studies me. "If you want anything from him you will have to meet him at the level he is capable of."

"He left me. I don't owe him a thing."

"Your choice," she says, pushing the forkful of cardamom cake into her mouth.

My aunt is extremely annoying all the time. "You don't have to cut me off every time I say something. I just don't want to deal with him."

"It's your choice."

"How many times are you going to dismiss me?"

"The thing I've realized about this family," she says, thinking, "is how often we deflect. Have you noticed that about us?" I turn away, annoyed. Of course I have. "You don't owe him a thing, but maybe you owe yourself something. You could forgive him and then maybe he would open up about who he is. And you would open up about who you are."

I cringe. "I don't want to know who I am."

"No. You've made that clear."

"But you know?"

She slices through her date nut cake with a polished knife and drops a piece onto her plate. An escaping cloud of powdered sugar explodes all over the table. "I know who you are. Yes."

"I'm a girl."

Georgia laughs. "Good one."

"Born into a family of weirdos!"

"Born into a family of archivists," she says, correcting me.

"Archivists?"

"We're preservationists," she tries. "Preserving the past."

I look around the room crowded with fading antique books, dark dusty Victorian furniture, chipped glass vases, an umbrella stand filled with rotting silk umbrellas, a carriage wheel, a green parrot feather under glass, and a couple of dried moth carcasses pinned to a board. I wheeze, "We're collectors of dead things, Georgia."

"We're historians unable to part with the past, but when has the past been bad?" I look away. "Think about it, Meg. The past might have been bad for some. It might have been good."

I take a bite of cardamom cake. "My past was OK," I admit. "Until it wasn't."

"Maybe." She scrutinizes the date nut cake and frowns. "Maybe the past wasn't so good for your father. He was always playing second fiddle to your mother's desires."

I blow on the fire to encourage it to burn. "I don't want to talk about him."

"She was very determined to right those wrongs that Sir Barrie..."

"I said I don't want to talk about it."

"If she could have, she might have changed a few minds about our responsibility to this planet. We're stewards. And the Darling women have a lot to say about the faerie realm."

"You don't have to tell me Dad thinks I'm meant to be a writer. That I'm supposed to follow in Mom's footsteps. That I'm..." I shoot her a look of concern. "I'm not doing it."

"You're you," she offers. "You're not your mom. But if you don't think you belong here..."

"What's that supposed to mean?"

Georgia hands me a slice of date nut cake on another china plate. "Here, try this one. It's a new recipe." I push it away. "It means you're the daughter of a woman who comes from a long line of strong independent women. Women who once worked the land, who rode horses and plowed fields. Women who helped build these clapboard houses alongside their husbands and uncles and cousins, who lived without electric heating and plumbing, who helped raise barns, who grew their own food, who canned, baked bread, raised families..."

"I get it."

"Women who lived off the land and contributed to its preservation." She folds her hands in prayer. "We owe them our gratitude, Megan Elida Fay. We don't know these women anymore. We think we do, but women today," she admits, "we're disconnected from our past." She lifts a finger. "Don't forget, Meg. You're a Darling."

"No, I'm not. Dad gave me a different name."

Georgia is quiet for a moment, thinking. "But don't you want to know who your mother was?"

"She wasn't some character in a storybook. I know that."

"She was an emblem of grace under pressure."

"What do you mean?" I ask annoyed.

"You are your mother's daughter, a Darling, and your father, well, he's an outlier to the Darling magic. And he knows this. I imagine he wanted to experience the faerie realm. Badly."

"We need to move on from the past, Georgia."

"You could have had that magic yourself if you weren't so stubborn, but because you didn't go, didn't want to go, can't go, your father has nothing left to want from you. He doesn't need you. And this is the reason he's become aloof. You can ask yourself--do you need him?"

"What about you? You're an outlier."

"I'm an interloper," she admits. "I thought I could have had access to the magic, but I was wrong." I don't want to hear this, but I turn to her and ask why. "You tell me," she tries.

I'm getting angry. "Georgia, you're the reason I didn't see Peter," I shout. "You're the..."

"You're the reason you didn't see him."

"How can you say that?" I cry. "You're the one who pushed Theo into the closet. When I heard her scream like that I came running back downstairs so, of course, I didn't see him. You ruined everything!" I yell. "You're the reason I lost my best friend!"

"You're the reason she stays away."

Eleven

It took months for Georgia to admit she forced Theo into the closet that night. And when she did, she told me it was because it wasn't Theo's magical night. It was mine. She was afraid that if Theo didn't get out of the way Peter Pan wouldn't make himself available to me, and if he didn't make himself available, centuries of faerie magic would be lost from the Darling home. She said she did it to protect me. My dad has corroborated her story and has been begging me to go to the attic tonight, the night of my seventeenth birthday, and try again. Never! Georgia was wrong and I hate her for ruining my friendship with Theo. But I am the one who failed my mother and my grandmothers. Georgia has made that very clear.

Nothing about the night of my sixteenth birthday makes sense. In truth, both Theo and I could have gone to Fable Island if Georgia hadn't pushed her into the closet. If I saw the island, and Theo saw Peter Pan, then it stands to reason that Georgia is the one living in doubt. Not us.

I push the chair in under my desk and turn to exit the class-room quickly, but Ms. Park says, "Meg, can I see you for a moment?" I cringe. She's been too nice to me lately and I'm not sure I understand why. I look at the door thinking I should leave and pretend I didn't hear her, but when she calls my name again, I stop. "It's only been a year, but it feels more like a century since your sophomore year. Now look at you—AP Biology. You're getting along just fine, aren't you?" I nod. She looks down at my new boots. "With everything you've got going for you, your test scores, and the advanced classes, I hope this will improve your chances of getting a good scholarship." I nod again. "How many colleges will you be applying to?"

I turn to look out the classroom window. "Two."

She raises her eyebrows just like Theo used to do. "Only two?" I turn, look her in the eye, and nod. "You've turned a corner in your life, haven't you? I won't keep you," she says, indicating the door with a nod of her head, "but we should talk about your choices. I can help with the college essay. I have some ideas. Come by and talk to me anytime. I admire you." I smile weakly. "Your situation. You. You've been exceptionally disciplined ever since the start of your junior year. Your aunt tells me..."

I turn on my heels. "I have to go, Ms. Park."

"Yes, of course. Happy birthday, Meg," she says smiling.

I turn from her and frown. She has no idea who I am. "If I get into Harvard," I reply, waltzing toward the door, "I'll let you know."

I imagine her eyes widen. "Oh my," she says uneasily. "*Bon chance.*"

The walk home from school is wet and cold, and my new boots slip on the snowy sidewalk. I wish I had worn a sturdier pair. Rubber-soled boots are ridiculous footwear for a Maine winter, yet everyone thinks they're the best. It's a slow walk. I turn off South Street, my pack heavy with textbooks hitting the small of my back, and take the shortcut through a vacant lot before turning again to make my way over a well-worn bicycle path and through a meadow. From the top of the hill overlooking the Atlantic Ocean, I see a succession of gray waves hitting the rocky beach. They roll and pitch predictably, no differently than they did last year, except this time I see only open water. Nothing more. I can just make out the kittiwake almost stopping mid-flight as she struggles against the wind and pauses before letting go and allowing the receding wind to push her along.

Theo doesn't come to school anymore. If we were still friends I know she would. Her mom says she's happier at home, but I don't know. I no longer call in the hope she'll answer. I wish I had been a better friend, I think, watching the gull slip through a bank of clouds. If anything still haunts me about my birthday, it is the loss of both my mom and my best friend. Without them, it just isn't worth celebrating. "Maybe the past isn't so good after all, Mom," I realize, slipping down the path.

I laugh when I think about Harvard. Of course I won't get in. That's the whole point. Maybe, like my dad, I am defiant after all, and the act of applying someplace as unattainable as Harvard is the whole point of being a renegade spirit. Maybe that's what I am. Can I be a renegade deliberately defying what is expected of me? Of all the stupid ideas. Harvard! I can't help but laugh out loud. There's no way I will get in, but I will apply to both

Harvard and Yale for the fun of it. Me. Megan Elida Fay. A Darling.

I cross the street and hurry to the beach down a broken set of steep wooden stairs, now twisted and buckling from last year's nor'easter. If I could turn back the clock one, possibly eleven years, I would, but I can't. I pick up a handful of pebbles and toss them into the waves. "Go," I whisper uneasily. "I don't need you." I reach for another handful of stones. "I will miss you, Mom, but I can't do this anymore." The waves break easily, rhythmically, and in succession. Impatiently, I toss the pebbles. "I can't stay here. I need someplace of my own." The kittiwake appears momentarily over the break in the waves but then disappears again through a thickening veil of clouds. "I'll finish school. I've promised myself that. If only to say that I didn't fail, but after that…"

I turn around suddenly, maybe wanting her to show herself one last time, but my mom is not here, and the older I become, and the farther away I get from my six-year-old self, the lonelier this feels. "Go," I plead when the kittiwake reappears through the clouds. "Please leave. I can't keep coming down here every day hoping something will change."

I turn from the gull and clamber back up the twisted stairs to the house, pausing as I walk past the small cemetery at the top of the hill. Surrounded by a toppling iron fence needing more than just a new coat of black paint, the unkept graveyard is crowded with aging stones. These are not just our family's graves, but the graves of most of the people who once lived nearby. I can't make out their names on the dirty granite stones because they have become worn and illegible, but it's not hard to see Mom's polished stone sticking out like a lighthouse beacon among them. It was placed next to my grandmother's stone which sits next to Grandad's. Behind them, as though supporting their backs, are my great-grandparents' graves. And behind those lie my great-great-grandparents' graves. "I have to leave you, Mom. There's nothing left for me here."

I know what her tombstone says. I don't need to read it again so I hitch my pack up onto my shoulder and turn away defiantly. *Without an appreciation for Beauty, this earthly life is inconceivable.* But I choke on the words. The passage is from *Fable Island,* words my father chose for her for all eternity. I scamper over the frozen ground thinking about how her tombstone will shine brightest among the rest for as long as it is there.

Pushing on the back door, and stepping into the dark oak kitchen, I kick off my boots and slip silently into the room. Georgia turns from the farmhouse sink, now stained by the many generations of Darling women who once stood there and put up all kinds of jams and jellies. She reaches for a dish towel and wipes her hands. "We're having lasagna."

"I don't want it."

"But it's your favorite."

"It's wrong. I don't want it."

"I've worked hard."

I sneer. "For you. Not for me."

"How dare you!"

I shift my backpack farther up onto my shoulder and push past her. I don't want to deal with Georgia. Not now. We'll just get into another argument about how she's right and I'm wrong. Inevitably, she will ask me about Theo. She always does.

"Friends support one another," she will argue. "Call her. It's your birthday." And then I will explain, like I always do, that I was the one who didn't support Theo so of course she is mad. Then Georgia will remind me that Theo is young, and once more the conversation will somehow circle back to Georgia and how supportive she is of Theo, how proud she is of her, and how I must be the strong and understanding one. Something like that. My head spins every time I think of the ways Georgia complicates things.

"Young lady!" she barks. I turn to face her, defiant. "This came in the mail for you today," she says, pushing a large brown envelope into my hands.

"If it's from Dad I don't want it."

"Take it. It's for you," she says uneasily. I snatch the envelope and turn to go. "We'll talk about it after you've read it."

I look down at the return address: Thailand. "You opened it?" I shriek.

"It's addressed to me," she answers.

I scowl. Sure enough, the envelope is addressed to Georgia Darling. "What is it?"

"I believe it's your birthday present," she says, running her hands through her hair and tucking a few gray wisps behind her ear. "I don't know why I was the recipient. I thought maybe it was your father's will if you want to know the truth. It's not a will," she says carefully. "Open it."

The envelope has been torn in places while making its long journey here and is haphazardly repaired with Priority Mail tape. I turn it over and stare at my father's handwriting. The address is written in all caps and the letters are almost illegible because his hand trembles. "What am I supposed to do with these?" I ask, slipping a stack of brittle papers out of the envelope.

"There's no note," she says, "but it's obvious what it is."

On the first page, I read the following words: *THE FAERIES OF FABLE ISLAND* by Wendy M. Darling. "This is my mom," I whisper.

Georgia is crying. "And your grandmother. And your great-grandmother. And," she says, the tears catching in her throat, "your great-great-grandmother. You know your mother, and her mother, and her mother before her…"

"Were all named Wendy."

"You're a Darling," says Georgia, quickly wiping away the tears with the back of her hand. "These are their stories. And this," she says, with her hand shaking, "is what they saw when they went to the island."

I turn the papers over in my hands. "Look! This is their handwriting!"

"They all went," she says, unable to hold back more tears. "And to see this. Now, after all these years. I had no idea this manuscript even existed. Or that your father had it. No idea he took it from her. From me. From us." She looks me in the eye. "This," she says, continuing to battle back the tears, "is the truth."

"It belongs to you, Georgia," I offer, pushing the manuscript into her hands. "It was addressed to you. It was meant…"

"It was meant for the two of us, Meg," she says, softening and pulling me into an embrace. "Please read it. Maybe we can find equanimity once and for all."

Together, we sift through the yellowing pages. Not only my mother, but my grandmother, my great-grandmother, and my great-great-grandmother, each with their elaborate scrolling letters, have contributed to the manuscript. Their ink-stained words are difficult to read. "I don't understand. Is this what Peter Pan…" I cough, hardly believing what I'm about to say. "Is this what the story of Peter Pan was supposed to be?"

Georgia shakes her head. She looks sad. "Honestly, I don't know, Meg. Your mother might have been able to answer that. Or Gramma. But we're on our own here."

I turn over the first page and read aloud, "*Gentle Reader, some will dismiss me as foolish, others as sentimental or brazenly irresponsible, but without these words, the passion I am about to share will be forfeited to the wind. We are not industrialized machines wringing our hands to and fro creating our desires, rather we are but simple levers and fulcrums unable to keep pace with humanity's ways. But on Fable Island, yes, Dear Reader, the illustrious island of Professor Yardley's persuasion where all who believe in the faerie realm will rightly pass, I have seen with my own eyes the simple truth.*" I stumble over the cursive handwriting and hand the paper to Georgia. "What does this say?"

"*There are those who will teach humanity the strength of our desire for it lies not in this industrialized world, but in the landscape of knowledge called Fable.*" She laughs. "That's a mouthful."

"Here, let me try," I offer, turning to the next page. "Look! There's a drawing of a faerie in the margin."

Georgia grins. "Look at the way the holly leaves fold in on themselves to create her gown. That's amazing detail on such a small illustration."

"*Were it not for man's erroneous ways,*" I continue, "*the simple spirits of this fabled island would burst forth for all to see and teach the magic of their hidden realm, and then you, Dear Reader, would be spared humanity's curse. There is magic, and the industrious Faerie Queen will forever give us her codes were we to listen and observe.*"

"Go on," says Georgia, slipping off her soiled apron and sitting down in one of the kitchen chairs. She closes her eyes.

"Someone has made a notation on the page. It's written in purple ink. It says, *Simplify this.* Could that have been Mom?"

"Let me see," says Georgia excitedly. "Yes! That's her handwriting."

"You told me she was writing a book. Do you think this was it?"

"I knew she was working on a book, but I had no idea about all this. Your mother and father were rather secretive about it."

"Then why did he...?"

"Send it to you?" She looks deliberately into my eyes, and as if stating the obvious, she says, "He needs you, Meg." I bristle. "Don't doubt it, child. There's magic. And it's time someone told it straight."

"Then why wasn't I named Wendy like Mom and Gramma? And my great-grandmothers?" I ask. "If I'm a Darling."

Georgia shakes her head. "I don't know. Perhaps your father..."

"He was jealous. Maybe he made Mom take his name when they married so he could keep the faerie magic for himself and then he made me..."

"No. That doesn't make sense. He wanted you to have this," says Georgia. "He was the one who knew the stories and encouraged you and your mother."

"He wanted the faerie magic all for himself, Georgia, and by not giving me the name Wendy Darling, he thought that would make it possible for him to go to the island. And then when he couldn't get there, just like Sir Barrie who failed to find the island, and Mom died, he panicked. He left me. He failed. But then I failed," I realize, dropping down into another one of the kitchen chairs. "I failed my dad."

Georgia reaches out and takes ahold of my hands. "No. Your father loves you. You're his darling. If anyone failed you..."

I push her away. "He ruined everything, Georgia."

"No," she responds. "He faltered. People falter, Meg. All the time. Your mother loved your name," she says, taking hold of my hands again. "She was proud of its faerie origin and proud of who you would be. She never would have given you a different name if she thought it would hurt your chances of going to Fable Island. You're Megan Elida Fay, our faerie child."

"This changes everything."

"What do you mean?"

"I'm mad," I hiss, standing and turning from her. "I'm so mad at my mom for dying. And now there's this manuscript. You keep it. It's too much. I have to let her go."

"Honestly, Meg," she offers, "I don't think the name matters. Our grandmothers all kept the Darling name even when they married, as did I. But for them it was symbolic. Times were different then. Think how unprecedented that would have been. But they represented the magic of Fable Island and they knew it."

I just want to hit something. "We've become a storybook character."

"That people love, Meg. Please don't lose sight of that."

"But she's not real!"

Georgia sighs. "Let's read this together and then you can decide how you feel. At least your father has returned it. And now we can say he did the honest thing. A little late, but…"

"I should have been a Wendy," I cry. "Then I would know what I'm supposed to do. But I can't write a book when no one believes in me."

"Shhh, sweetheart. You've had enough tears. No more," she tries. "I didn't say you had to write anything. But let's read this. It's time you learn the truth about Fable Island."

I turn to the kitchen window. Rising temperatures throughout the day have begun to melt the snow, producing a kind of dense fog that permeates the shoreline with a low-lying veil of moisture. It closes in around the house, obscuring everything in a thick cloud. "I need to get out of here," I complain.

Georgia's voice sounds worried. "And go where?"

"Nowhere. Everywhere. I can't stay here."

"But this is your home," she tries.

"No, it's your home. Their home," I cry, pointing to the kitchen table where ancient stories spill out from a fading manuscript. "Where everyone dies."

"Come on, Meg, You can't be serious. This is as much your home as it was theirs. We're Darlings. This is who we are."

"No. It's not who I am. My father made sure of that."

"That's not true."

"It's who you want me to be, but I'm not a Wendy," I shout, throwing my hands into the air. "Maybe Dad was right. Maybe he tried on the name for me and it didn't fit. Maybe these ghosts," I shudder, "need to go. You're holding onto her, Georgia. We both are. We need to let Mom go."

"But if we let her go…"

"Then we free her. We free ourselves," I shout.

"Where are you going?"

"I can't stay here."

"But it's your birthday!"

"I need to talk to Theo," I explain. "She was right." Georgia folds her hands in prayer. "She wasn't right about you. Or this," I say, indicating the sagging kitchen floor in need of new joists. "She was right about moving on." I thrust my feet into my boots, grab my backpack, and pull on the door. "Don't wait up for me."

"You will get lost in this mist," she says nervously.

"I'm going over to Theo's. I know the way."

Twelve

Naturally, one would think that something untoward would happen to me at this point, as this is the direction most stories take about this time. Then how can this be a fairy tale if something true happens? And why I am the one caught between what is real and what is make-believe? No one sees imaginary islands or lives in a falling-down house filled with the memories of four generations of Darling women who may or may not have seen Peter Pan. But what I will experience won't be what Sir Barrie experienced. This, I will learn, is the magic of Fable Island.

I run down the beach path on my way to Theo's because I do, at this point, think I'm going to go to her and beg forgiveness, but what happens next is true. I see a narrow wire footbridge suspended high above the water. The emerald green paint is peeling and the bridge is sagging with age. "Shit," I exclaim. "I don't believe it!" When the veil of clouds, which had been obscuring the top of the suspension bridge, moves, I can just make out the teetering apex. "Shit, shit, shit. That's high," I realize. "Are you serious? This is the bridge to Fable Island?" I throw my backpack down onto the beach. "It's ancient." The kittiwake glides easily through the wires and then disappears again. "Damn that bird," I curse. "Who are you?"

"Mom?" I call. "Peter?" No answer. "This can't be real." I turn my back on the bridge and count 1-2-3. There's no way I'm going over that thing. "Is anyone here?" Again, no answer. "Do you want me to believe you're real, Peter? Is that the game?" I turn around again and stare up at the aging wires. They don't look like much. They certainly don't look strong enough to hold a person willing to walk across the metal frame. "Who built this?" I shout. I throw a few round stones at the bridge, and when they hit the metal they clang, reverberating loudly before falling into the water. I can just make out three concentric circles when the stones hit the surface.

Not one tourist coming here wanting to find the bridge has ever found it. They have waited and watched and prayed and hoped, but for over a hundred and thirty years, this scene has not played out. "Peter?" I shout. "Is this the bridge my mom saw?" No answer. "Are you showing up?" Again, nothing. "How do you expect me to believe in you if you don't show yourself?"

I toss another small rock at the bridge, and when it bounces off a metal piling and hits the surface of the water, I hear a kerplunk. I turn around and look up at our weathered house. Maybe Georgia will see this too and come running down to the beach, but the house is still and lonely. The kittiwake sits on the pitched roof where silvered gray lichens, in various stages of decay, cling to the asphalt shingles. She cocks her head and looks down at me until she seems spooked by something, throws out her wings, and hops. Quickly, she lifts herself with the wind, dives down to the ground, catches the wind again, and flies up over the cottage. I turn around again. The bridge is still there.

If the bridge is real, and I am real, and the beach is real, and the sound of my voice is real, then Fable Island should, by all deductive reasoning, be real. Then my mother and my grandmothers, who were real, and who wrote their experiences on real pieces of paper, created something true. But then why didn't Sir Barrie see the bridge? And why didn't my great-great-grandmother just give him the truth so he could write it real? Why did he take this away from her and turn it into make-believe?

"Prof. Yardley?" I try. "How come you saw the bridge but my dad never did?" No answer. "Is this bridge only available to women?" Again, no answer. "That doesn't make sense. None of this makes sense. Peter? Are you here?"

This is the moment when all time, which we think of as our reality, ceases to exist. If I am at the beach on the afternoon of my seventeenth birthday, but I was supposed to see this one year ago, how is it that I am seeing it now? What happened to the wavelength? I laugh uneasily. That's a riddle I can't answer. I'm not very good at physics. The wind changes direction and moves the veil again so the bridge becomes obscured in cloud cover. All I can see are the first three rusted rungs of a ladder I will need to climb to access the bridge and cross the open channel. "No way!" I shout, throwing my hands through my wind-swept hair. "I can't even see the island."

This is not the right bridge. It looks dangerous. "Why," I cry, using one of Georgia's favorite expressions, "have I been tasked with this?" I stop to listen for a response. "How am I going to cross a rickety old bridge that goes on forever and doesn't land anywhere?" No answer. "Hello?"

Somewhere in the muddle between space and time, there is an equation we're supposed to use to access what is true. Can a person observing a questionable phenomenon step far enough away from it to properly discern what is true or what is false? Where, in time, will I be able to go to decide what is true if I can't escape space to become an objective observer? Can the time it takes for a person to observe something like a magical island, or a disused bridge on the verge of collapse, render the truth absolute? My observations might be these, but my father's observations were something different. How can we determine the truth if everyone perceives the same view differently? Do we live in a parallel time where observed realities are only true to the person who is experiencing them?

I laugh painfully. "What's the point of going? Will I meet the good faerie or the wicked one? Should I click my heels three times when I want to go home?" I swear this is a story. It has to be. And I am trapped between knowing. I turn to look up at the apex. It's so high I can't even see the other side. "I'm not going over that thing. I can't!"

Sensible people confronted with a dilemma such as this will turn around and walk away. Characters in a story defy logic and put their cold hands on rusted iron railings and take the first step. I can't help but take another step and then another. Pausing on the iron filigree step and looking down at the churning water below, I think, what if there isn't another side? At one time this bridge was beautiful, with delicately designed scrollwork, but now it is covered in slime. Over time, hundreds of sharp gray barnacles have attached themselves to the rusted pilings. They cling in various stages of growth, some small and others large. Many are piled one on top of the other. "Is this the bridge my mother used?" No answer. "My grandmothers?" I backtrack for a moment and step down from the ladder and back onto the beach. "Where are you, Peter?!"

If Fable Island is real and exists in the minds of some, but not in others, what does that say about humanity? I take another step backward. I need a better bridge, I realize. I don't trust this one. But what if this is the only bridge to Fable Island? And this is my only chance to go? There are definitely more questions than answers and there is no one here to help me. "Is this a joke?" I shout. I can't help but think about the trunk filled with my great-great-grandmother's long heavy skirts, lace petticoats, and wide-brimmed hats. At least I can wear pants while climbing it, I think, stumbling over the beach stones.

But I don't want to go, I realize, taking another step back. What's the point? I don't need Mom's dream. And I don't want the responsibility of keeping *Fable Island* or writing another book about it. I'm not a Wendy. I'm no one. "Please make it go away."

The kittiwake pulls through the air, and with a single target in her sights comes careening down the beach, flies low over the waves, pulls up into the air, circles, and returns. She lands beside me and hops on one foot, inching closer. But when I put out my hand she hops backward, unsure, and decidedly in fear. We don't feed the gulls on our beach so they are not used to us. They are often afraid. I point to the bridge. "Do you see that?" I ask. She turns away and pecks the ground. "It's the bridge to Fable

Island," I explain, sitting down beside her. She skitters away before resuming her search for mollusks. "I'm supposed to go, but it's not real." The kittiwake scurries toward the wet shoreline, and continuing her search for dinner, ignores me. "I'm afraid," I confess. "What if I don't go? Then what? Will I regret it for the rest of my life?" Without hesitating, the kittiwake lifts her wings, pumps them up and down several times to lift herself off the ground, and disappears through the veil. I watch her go.

"Peter?" I try. "Aren't you supposed to take me over that thing?" Again, no answer. "Are you real or are you only in the storybooks?" I can't help but laugh at myself, and hitching my backpack up onto my shoulders, I stand. "What the fuck. I'll go. I can't wait for you. It's cold out here."

My rubber-soled boots slip on the first step and that's when I confirm that the bridge is real. I stamp my feet to make sure the bridge feels solid, grab ahold of the railings, and hoist myself up. "Gentle Reader," I manage, holding on for dear life as my boots continue to slip on the seaweed-covered treads, "come with me." I tighten both hands around each of the railings and inch my way up. With each step, I feel like I'm making a mistake. Who does this? Those who believe? I continue taking the steps one at a time, and each time I put my boots on the treads, tighten my grip, and hoist myself up, I have to ask myself, "What is it you believe in, Meg?" I shake my head. I don't know. No one ever told me what to believe in, only that I was to believe in the faerie realm. "What has that ever done for me?!" I shout.

The trek is slow going and I can't see a thing, but it's as if the bridge and the mist and the miracle of magic all come together and take me up and over. Before I know it I'm approaching the top. "Now what?" I shout. "Will this lead me to Fable Island or will it dump me into the ocean?" No answer. "Am I really on the bridge or is this the part of the story where I wake up from a dream?" No. There are plenty of endings that don't involve dreams. That's a writer's cop-out. I need my life to be true and not make-believe. "Damn you, Sir Barrie," I curse, stepping into the unknown. "Too many people want the fairy tale. But this isn't one, is it?"

Thirteen

Obsidian-colored mussel shells with faded iridescent centers lie broken and discarded on the beach as though the gulls, who once dropped these shells on the smooth round rocks to open them and feast on their tender insides, had long ago left Fable Island in search of another. Entrails of seaweed, now dry and brittle, like the forgotten black ribbons on our beach, litter the ground. Thousands of storm tides have pushed the seaweed up to the edge of the woods where hollow logs, dried twigs, and a plastic bottle of some kind poke through the debris.

Hesitant to step off the bridge, I scan the narrow beach. The desolation is acute. There is nothing here. Empty of color, and devoid of life, the island feels like it is struggling to breathe. I have never seen a land this close to death, where everything looks lifeless and gray. The cathedral-like pines growing along the edge of the jagged granite rocks are battered, bent, burned, and missing branches. They are barely alive. Perhaps I've arrived on one of the 4,600 islands that lie off the Maine coast, but I don't know. This is not a healthy place.

First navigated by members of indigenous tribes who hunted for food along these shores, and later mapped when European fur traders arrived, our islands have all been found and the waters charted. Could it be that I'm not on Fable Island but on some other desolate unknown island?

"Hello!" I shout. "Am I here?" I need to make another decision, I think, tightening my grip on the handrails. Do I step off the bridge? What if it disappears and I can't get home? What if I find myself caught between time? "This is me," I shout to no one, to anyone who might be listening. "I'm not a Wendy!" The air is warm and I peel off my down vest and stuff it into my backpack. "Am I on Fable Island?"

I turn around and scan the bridge. I am not aware that the trek was difficult, but I do wonder how I did it. I climbed by carefully putting one foot in front of the other and when I came down the other side, I simply arrived. It was rather unremarkable. I scan the beach again, and in truth, it, too, is unremarkable. There is no sign that anyone lives here, although if this is Fable Island then I know the faerie magic isn't on the beach. It lies deep within the woods where Prof. Yardley first encountered the hidden realms. I laugh impatiently. Who is going to believe me? But why, all those years ago, did tourists believe in a faerie realm and come from all over the world hoping for a glimpse of it? Times have changed, I realize. People no longer believe in magic. *The minds of those who stifle creativity stifle the truth,* Prof. Yardley once wrote. *The feebleminded ones who don't trust themselves simply die.*

Maybe if I had read my grandmother's manuscript I would have known what to expect, but the island is a major disappointment. According to Mom's description, there were supposed to be rare flowering trees, colorful exotic flowers, and black granite rocks so polished that you could see your reflection in them. I wasn't expecting to come alone; I should have been escorted and shown the way. Maybe I should go back and beg Theo to come with me. I will go to her and promise never to distrust her again. I will tell her I need her. She will help me find Peter Pan, and together, we will find the hidden realm. I am about to turn around, deciding this is best, when the bridge melts away from me. I stumble over the wet rocks and onto the beach as though the thought of leaving pushed me into staying. "Shit," I cry, watching the bridge disappear into the mist. "What you'd go and do that for?"

My pack is filled with books. It is heavy and I curse myself for bringing it along, but how could I have left it behind? I always carry *Fable Island* with me everywhere I go. Leaving it at home isn't an option. "Is this real?" I shudder, scanning the horizon and looking back the way I came. "This better be real or else I'm..." I stop and tear through my backpack remembering I have a cell phone. Naturally, I don't have service but I can take pictures. Thank God for that. If only I had thought of this while I was on the bridge. If I had, I would have been able to prove that Fable Island was real, but I wasn't thinking straight. I know the pictures will look like any other forlorn beach, but I take a few photos to prove I'm here.

The sun is bright in a cloudless sky and the beach is hot. I shed my flannel shirt and tie it around my waist. Did my grandmothers take off their tight-fitting wool jackets when they arrived, or being modest, as they were expected to be, did they keep them on? I scan the beach for any sign of the bridge. "Peter?" I shout, "Am I supposed to wait here?" No answer. I need something to drink, I realize, looking toward the woods. I know I don't have a water bottle with me, but I open the pack again to check. No water. No snacks. "Hello?" I shout, shielding my eyes from the sun. "If you put me here you could help me!"

Out of desperation, I scurry to the comfort of the shady woods where I reach for my phone again and text Georgia. *I made it. Fable Island is real.* I hit send, but the message fails to deliver. "What happens now?" I shout. No answer. I check my phone again. No service. "I have a notebook," I explain. "I don't know if you want me to write anything down, but I will. Is this what you want me to do?" Even the woods are beginning to feel hot and muggy. I take off my T-shirt and adjust the straps on my sports bra, which has become soaked with perspiration. This isn't the island I was expecting, I realize. It's dying.

I scan the woods. There is a narrow deer trail leading away from the shore, and as the sun continues to bear down oppressively, I decide to follow it so that I can retreat further into the woods for more shade. But the path is overgrown with sharp thorns that get caught on my jeans. "This is fucked," I manage. "Now what? Are you coming for me?" No answer. "Peter! I can't just stay here and wait. Am I supposed to go into the woods and find you?" Dumping the heavy textbooks out of my pack and onto the ground, I turn and follow the overgrown trail through the dense dry foliage. I stop when the brittle leaves suddenly shift direction. "Who's there?" I shudder. "Anyone?"

This is not the time to panic. I'm too smart for that. If I was going to panic it would have been when I saw the bridge. But I didn't panic then and I'm not going to panic now. "Why exactly am I here?" I shout, dropping the pack to the ground. Perhaps it was a lark, a folly, a happenstance. These are not my words, but ones that Georgia uses, and I repeat them. Theo was right. I do use grown-up words. Maybe that's what the women of our persuasion do. After all, we're Darlings. Or I should have been, I realize, but my mother and father decided to make me different. "I know you're here." No answer. "And you're testing me." I throw my hands onto my hips. "This isn't fun," I shout. "Isn't coming here supposed to be fun?" Again, no answer.

I don't know why I suddenly feel sad, but I do. Perhaps it's the emptiness of it all. "I don't want this," I try. "There's nothing here." Maybe when I was younger and I believed in fairy tales, I imagined something exciting, but recalling the stories Mom once shared, this is bleak in comparison. Where is the golden rainbow? The field of transparent poppies? The wings? I reach behind me, but there's nothing there. "I was supposed to get wings," I try, pushing down the tears. I check my phone again, but there's still no service. "I'm ready to go home," I beg. "Please take me home." I text Theo. *I made it to Fable Island. Plz believe me. I'm sorry about everything.* "Hello?" I shout when the leaves turn over again. "If this is really happening, where are you?"

I continue walking, but the deer trail merges into another forgotten trail, and as they crisscross one another, I realize there's no way to know where to go. This is not a marked trail with signage. It is a tangled mess of paths that will either lead me somewhere or keep me going in circles. "Think, Meg," I hiss. "You're going to get blisters wearing these wet socks. And then what?" I'm getting mad at myself. I should have stayed on the beach. I turn around and retreat. Going through the woods was a stupid idea. "Stupid stupid stupid," I hiss. "I'm not doing it." But the labyrinthian deer trails and the wind and the cathedral-like pines are unimpressed by my cries. "Please," I whisper. "I'm not Wendy. This isn't fun."

Retreating to the beach, where I'm certain I should see the bridge, I shout, "OK. Game over. I'm ready to leave!" The heat is oppressive. I kick off my boots, peel the perspiration-soaked wool socks off my chafed feet, wriggle out of my jeans, and fling myself headfirst over the limp waves. The ocean water is thick with tangled muck. It is not refreshing and cool, but weighty and warm. I think about my choice of words. Weighty? Perhaps I should say the salt water is thick with brown algae, the ocean floor muddy with deep silt, and churning it up as I have only tangles the ribbons of black seaweed around my body. I hurl myself out of the water and throw myself down onto the beach, spitting out the alkaline taste of salt water. "Gross," I gag. "That's disgusting."

Scanning the beach again for any sign of something, I throw my wet socks over one of the bleached logs. I'm not interested in leaving this lookout or putting the socks back on, but if I do leave, they will need to be dry. Walking in wet socks will be disastrous. I will only get blisters. I lay out the rest of my clothes, open the boots, remove the insoles, and lay these out on the log as well. Sitting down uneasily in my purple underwear and sports bra, I'm convinced I'll just have to wait. "Are you coming for me?" I ask again. "If you're coming, then please, let's get this over with." No answer. I throw a rock into the air. This isn't right, I think. Something about this definitely isn't right.

I check my phone again and try to send Theo a photo of the rock-strewn beach, but it fails to go through. In the photo, the sun has obscured the woods in a brilliant light haze so the photo looks like one I might have taken on our beach. If only I had listened to Theo a year ago when she begged me to believe her, we could have come over together.

"He has transparent gossamer wings," she had said. "I promise he's here." Not only did I not believe her, I couldn't even pretend to believe her. Why didn't I just lie to her and tell her I trusted her? Because I can't lie. I don't know why, but I've never been able to put on the fake smile, the fake laugh, the fake anything. I'm not like most girls. And I never want to be like them. I want to be real.

"I'm leaving," I shout, standing abruptly and pushing the textbooks back into my pack. I scan the horizon for a boat or possibly a plane. Maybe someone has sent out a search party for me? But the ocean is still, too still, and the anemic waves show no signs of a wake. I peer into the cloudless sky. "Please," I manage. "Now what? I need to find something to drink."

My clothes have dried instantly in the heat, and I try stuffing them into my pack, but they don't fit so I dump the textbooks once again onto the ground. "Is that going to be a mistake?" I question, looking down at them. Without hesitating, I rip several pages from chapter three, *Abstractions of Time*, from my physics textbook, and stuff the torn pages into the side pockets of the pack. Wearing only my boy shorts, sports bra, dry socks, and rubber boots, I hitch the pack up onto my shoulders.

"I'll be back," I shout, walking down the beach in search of fresh water. "And then I want to go home."

There's something ridiculous about this whole thing. Think about it. I just crossed a wide ocean channel and landed on an island that isn't there. At least it's not there in the eyes of just about everyone who looks out across the Maine waters. And if a modern soul, someone who lives and breathes on this planet sometime around the year 2024, were to ever see an imaginary island they, well, let's just say they might get laughed at, or worse, discredited. "So what am I doing here? No one will believe this," I cringe. "Do I need to do something dumb and then redeem myself? Learn a lesson? Is that it?"

I flip my hair up onto the top of my head and secure the bun with an elastic band. "I know you're playing a game with me. It's what you do, isn't it, Peter?" Again, no answer. "You're going to have to show yourself soon because this is beginning to make me look like I'm helpless! And I am not helpless!" I hiss, dislodging the empty plastic bottle from the pile of debris. "Sprite?" I yell, looking at the faded green label. I throw myself down onto the beach and curse. "This is so fucked. Where the hell am I?"

And just like that the bridge appears. I look out across the water as it pushes itself up over the waves. Although it is still covered in a thick layer of slime, the clouds surrounding it have moved and I can now see the bridge in its entirety. "You've got to be kidding me." Not only does the apex appear twice as high as it did before, but the arc of the bridge appears to have lengthened. I don't think I can adequately describe how tall and long this bridge is. It must be twice as tall and twice as long as the Sydney Harbour Bridge in Australia. And how do I know this? Because I saw a photograph of it while researching bridge construction for a seventh-grade science project. It never occurred to me then, or later, that Georgia's interest in the construction of that particular bridge might have had something to do with the construction of this bridge. They look eerily similar.

Impulsively, I turn my back on the bridge and retreat into the woods. "I think something's wrong with me," I shudder. I dig my phone out of the pack and try calling Georgia, but the call fails. "This isn't Fable Island," I realize. "This is the future."

Fourteen

This isn't a dream. Dreams aren't real. And I promise, this is real. The sun burns my fair skin and turns it red. As the bridge weaves in and out of view like a distant mirage on a windswept dune, I try my phone again. "Come on, please," I whisper, "pick up." When Theo doesn't answer and the call fails, I shout, "I can't cross that bridge. It's too high. It's not real!"

I pick up my calculus textbook. Real, I think, holding it to my chest and flipping through it. I pause on page thirteen where I've written a note to myself in the margin that says, *You've got this.* I look up at the steel girders and think, do I? Calculus is difficult, but doable. I don't love it, but Ms. Park thought I should take it my junior year so I can take AP Calculus next year. "It's the best way forward into a good college, Meg," she promised. "You've got this." Now I'm not so sure.

I'm not going to college, I remind myself, scrutinizing the bridge. I toss the book to the ground where it flips on the stones and splays open. What would Grandad say he if saw me rip pages from a book and discard it like it meant nothing? If he saw me disrespectfully break the spine of another? He was so attached to his books that he would never just toss them aside, I realize, remembering the ornate antique ones with gold-embossed covers. Protected by clear plastic sleeves, the books soon overfilled the small shop, spilled out from the shelves, and lined the wobbly floors of The Book Galley. Most of his inventory sat in dusty piles and never sold, as they were all too expensive for tourists, he said. He would never let them go for less than what they were worth. After Grandad died and Georgia sold his shop, along with his collection of beautiful books, she decided to take the most valuable ones from his collection for herself.

"Your grandad would never forgive me if I didn't find the proper home for these," she said, pushing the heavy winter coats aside in the front hall closet to make room for the cardboard box of books. "We can't sell these. Not yet. They're our future."

I don't know if those books are worth anything. Maybe she knows that after all these years they've lost their value and this is why Georgia says she can't afford to send me to college. "I don't know and I don't care," I say, reluctantly peeling my eyes off the bridge and picking up the textbook. "If I'm going to go home now is my chance, but what if I don't get home? What if..." I shudder, grabbing the textbooks and piling them into my arms like a heavy load of firewood. But within a split second of my touching them, the textbooks crumble into microscopic particles like the dust covering Grandad's old books, and they float away with the wind. "No..." I whisper painfully, watching the books go. I grab my backpack to make sure *Fable Island* is still there. It is.

"Don't panic, Meg. You've got this." But the bridge continues to wobble. It's like an optical illusion of some kind, I realize, watching it go in and out of focus. I still don't know where I am. Maybe I'm on a magical fabled island, but then again, maybe I'm not. I grab the plastic Sprite bottle, fill it with thick dark ocean water, and secure the cap. I pick up a few smooth beach stones and put them into the pack. Struggling to pull on my stiff jeans, I think, what else can I bring home? I slip on my boots, scurry over the stones, grab a handful of seaweed, and climb the slippery bridge ladder. "1-2-3-4," I say, counting the steps while tightening my grip on the handrails. The beach stones hit the small of my back. "Real," I say, reminding myself of what should be obvious. But when I turn to look behind me, the island, like the textbooks, vanishes in a kind of obscure particle haze. I watch it go. "Get me the hell out of here," I curse, scrambling over the bridge.

And just like that, I'm back home.

Fifteen

"You're back early," says Georgia, jamming an oversized log into the woodstove. She looks past me and over my shoulder. "Did you bring Theo back with you for your birthday dinner?" I shake my head. "Aren't you cold?" she asks. "Where's your vest?"

"I ...it's in my pack," I explain, kicking off the wet boots and throwing black mud onto the kitchen floor.

"Boots!" she says pointing. But I ignore her as she takes a long look at me searching for irregularities. "It might snow tonight," she says, taking a deep breath, leaning over to pick up the muddy boots, and placing them on the boot tray. "What are you doing out there in just your sports bra? Where's your shirt?"

"I'm not OK, Georgia," I admit. "Something...something happened."

"Where have you been? Your hands are filthy."

I lift them toward the warm stove. "I don't know."

"And you smell," she says, lifting a tomato-stained dish towel off her shoulder and waving it in front of her face.

"I went swimming."

Alarmed, she shrieks, "Where?"

"I don't know."

"Do I need to call a doctor?" she asks, taking my arm and sitting me down in one of the spindly kitchen chairs. I shake my head. "What happened? Did you fall?" I continue to look at her, bewildered. I don't know how to tell her what happened. "What's your name?" she asks quickly. I ignore her. "Your name?" she repeats.

Annoyed, I answer, "Meg."

"Your full name and your Social Security number." I stare at her blankly. "Do you know your full name and number?" she asks, raising her voice. When she insists, I answer her. "Your mother's name?"

"Wendy Darling. I mean Fay."

"And your address?"

"111 Raspberry Lane. What just happened?" I ask. Georgia has a smudge of dried tomato sauce on her cheek. I can't take my eyes off it.

"Are you safe?" she asks, taking my hands in hers. "Did someone..."

"No. No one..."

"You weren't gone long. Ten minutes tops. Are you sure you didn't fall and hit your head?" she asks, looking me up and down.

"No." I glance through the open swinging door and into the dining room where she has placed three of my great-great-grandmother's blue china plates, three place settings of her English filigree silver, and three crystal goblets on the polished mahogany table. "I texted you."

Georgia can't take her eyes off me. "My phone's in the other room," she says, indicating the dining room. "Are you OK? Do you want me to call...?"

"No. Can you please check it?" I stammer, opening my pack. I pull out the heavy rocks, the wet seaweed, the bottle of sulfuric ocean water, and the stained copy of *Fable Island* and place them, one by one, onto the kitchen table. I toss the muddied white gloves onto the floor. Georgia gasps. "I need you to check your phone," I repeat, reaching for mine. Sure enough, my text to Georgia is still there and I resend it. "Please," I beg. "Did it go through?" She is stricken at the sight of the soiled copy of *Fable Island* but then turns toward the dining room where she has left her phone on the upright piano. "I don't know what happened, but I...something happened," I stammer while resending my text, along with the photos of the beach, to Theo. "I went somewhere."

She pulls the book to her chest and cradles it. "Look what you did!"

"I didn't do anything, Georgia," I manage. "I didn't do that."

"It's ruined!" she cries.

"I didn't ruin it. It's just...forget it!" I shout, taking the book from her. "What does the text say? I need to know what I wrote."

She looks again into the dining room and then at *Fable Island*. "I'll check," she answers carefully.

I hold my breath. "Please, please, please," I whisper, wrapping my trembling hands around the only copy of *Fable Island*.

When Georgia returns to the kitchen and shows me her phone we both take in a sharp bewildered breath before letting it out slowly. "Fable Island?" she says stumbling. I shake my head, uncertain. "No?"

With tears forming, I shudder, "I don't know."

"What do you mean?"

"It wasn't what I expected," I say, picking up the entrails of seaweed and the discarded plastic bottle. "It was ugly."

"Fable Island isn't ugly."

I bury my face in my hands, ashamed. "I know."

My phone chimes and Georgia looks at it. "It's Theo," she cries. "Oh thank God. She's coming over."

———

Acting uncharacteristically timid, Theo peers through the open door and into the kitchen. "Come in, sweetheart," says Georgia, frantically waving her inside.

"Is it true?" Theo asks, shaking off the cold and removing her worn rubber boots. She places them neatly on the boot tray, toes aligned as Georgia likes them, and steps into the warm room in her heavy wool socks. Our eyes meet. "I ran out the door the second I got your text."

Georgia takes Theo into her arms and hugs her. I close my eyes and wait for Theo to tell me what a horrible person I am, but she slides down onto one of the kitchen chairs and puts her hand on the table.

"I believe you," she says, offering me a translucent poppy that looks as though it has been dried and flattened. It is clear, almost like pressed glass, and looks just as fragile. "I put it inside a Bible. It's been there all this time. But it was meant for you." Our eyes meet. This time I let mine linger. "I took it from your room that night," she admits. "I should have returned it. I wanted to." The words form in my head and I want to tell Theo I'm the one who should be apologizing, but I can't get them to come out. I stare at the poppy. "Peter dropped it on the floor. I picked it up..."

"And kept it?"

She answers sincerely. "I'm sorry. It was wrong of me."

Georgia folds her arms over her chest. "There. Now that that's done."

Theo gasps when she sees the soiled copy of *Fable Island*. "What happened?!"

I look away. "I was trying to get home. I was worried if I didn't hold onto the book it might...vaporize."

Theo throws me a look of concern. "Vaporize?"

"I dropped it...it slipped from my hands," I explain, offering them up to her. "And it landed in the muck. There was a lot of seaweed."

Georgia is cautious when she says, "I don't understand. You have a responsibility toward this book..."

"The island is not what you think! It's not the same!"

"Are you even sure you went?" she asks.

I shake my head. "I just don't understand why it was so hot. It was decimated and void of any color. It looked like it was dying."

"You went to the wrong island," explains Georgia matter-of-factly.

I complain to Theo, "Why didn't you tell us about the poppy that night? We could have figured it all out then. Maybe I would have understood. I could have believed..."

Theo blushes. "I wanted it for the baby."

Georgia pulls up a chair and sits down beside Theo. "Your baby sister," she says, trying out the words, "would have wanted

Meg to have it. And as much as your heart was in the right place..."

"She knows, Georgia," I say annoyed.

"It's been bad. Ever since that night. And I didn't know how to come back," Theo explains. "It's all been just so bad. I wanted to..."

"You're here now," says Georgia.

Theo pulls me into her and hugs me. I let her hold me because we both need this but then she pulls away. "You stink."

Georgia says, "She went swimming."

"Where?"

"I don't know," I try. "It definitely wasn't the Fable Island I expected."

"Then what was it?" she asks.

I shake my head. "I don't know. This sample came from the ocean," I wince, handing Theo the bottle. "And the beach was littered with..."

Theo raises an eyebrow. "You found a Sprite bottle on Fable Island?"

Georgia waves her hand in front of her face. "Go shower, Meg."

Theo frowns. "It's OK, Georgia. We need to hear what happened."

"But the stench..."

Theo studies me for a moment, thinking. "The worst of the grief is behind you, Meg," she offers. "You're home." She buries her head in her hands. "But I understand now how you feel about your mom. I do. My mom's going to be all right, I know she will, and I'm helping as best I can, but it's bad. We named the baby

Poppy." She pauses. "She's buried in a casket...this big," she says, opening her arms no wider than the length of a doll's cradle.

I close my eyes and sigh. "Poppy. I love that name."

Georgia is quiet when she says, "We do know what you're going through, Theo. Your mom is lucky to have you."

"I'm lucky I have her too," she says crying. She turns to me. "I'm sorry."

"Meg and I have each other," Georgia offers. "And we're learning how to make that work."

I close my eyes. I know I will never be able to unsee the desolation of Fable Island. Images of a place now lost and ruined are all I will have left of my mom's dream. "I don't want to go back to the past. I need to move on." I say, stepping away from them. "It's obvious I can't keep *Fable Island*."

Georgia is abrupt. "You can't give up now."

"You have to go back," Theo cries, offering me the poppy. "Please. Can't you go back and make it better?"

"How?"

"You're a Darling, Meg," whispers Georgia. "Please. Go back. Maybe you took a wrong turn..."

"You don't understand!" I shout. "It was...like the future...and it was bad! The algae. The heat. It was..." I stop and look at the bottle of decomposing microscopic particle sludge. "I went somewhere really bad."

Georgia is nervous when she asks, "You can do that?"

"I think I bent time," I realize. "I must have stepped away from what we think of as time and into the reality of time." I shake the bottle. "This is the future...the heat...the algae."

"What do you mean?" asks Theo confused.

"I don't know," I answer truthfully. "All I know is I walked across a bridge to another land. I think I unlocked the future." Uneasily, I pull the torn textbook pages from my backpack. "I was going to use these for toilet paper," I admit, spreading them out onto the table, "but look at this. It's a drawing of a clock. No one knows what time really is. I mean, we think we understand time because we understand a linear past and a linear future, but somehow the idea of linear time doesn't work when we begin to study quantum mechanics. Time becomes a loop, a circle," I explain. "I don't believe we will ever really understand time until we understand the probability that time isn't real. We think we understand time, and we think that it is real, but maybe we're stuck in our thinking."

"What does this have to do with the faeries?" asks Georgia.

"They're real," Theo admits. "And we have to go back and find them!"

"They might want something," I concede. "I think their past is intersecting with our future."

"They have something to tell us," Theo explains. "We need to go."

I shake my head. "It was horrible, Theo. It was so hot and forlorn."

Georgia is adamant. "You have to return, Meg. For Poppy. For your mom and dad. For all of us."

"Please, Meg, I want to go with you," Theo begs. "We can make it better."

"I bent time," I say, exhaling excitedly. "I walked through the veil. This is what I will write about, Georgia. I will write about the loop."

"Can you do it again?" she asks. "And take Theo with you?"

Theo begs, "Tonight!"

"Exactly one year later," Georgia offers. "But if you think you can bend time…"

"Tonight," I conclude. "It has to be tonight. I don't know what Prof. Yardley would have said about time, but I would tell him he missed the whole point of Fable Island. It's not real."

Theo puts her hands on her hips. "But you just said…"

"I didn't say it didn't exist," I say laughing. "I said it's not real. And there's a huge difference." I look into their bewildered faces and clap my hands triumphantly. "Peter Pan exists and I will prove how Sir Barrie went to Fable Island and found him after all!"

Sixteen

Being overly protective, as she always is with Theo, Georgia straps one of Grandad's old headlamps onto her forehead. She tells her that because I already know the way across the bridge I won't need to see where I'm going, but that she will. Georgia points her flashlight out across the waves and jumps up and down on the beach saying she can't see the bridge, but both Theo and I promise her we can. I thrust my hands into the darkness and feel my way as we climb the slippery wet bridge in nothing but our T-shirts and shorts. When I can no longer hear Georgia shout, "Meg! Theo! Can you hear me? Make smart choices," I know that we have stepped across time.

Crossing the bridge isn't easy for Theo. It turns out that she's afraid of heights. Since she knew this about herself, and she knew she was going to walk over a rickety old bridge, I wish she had been better prepared. She could tighten her focus and accept the probability that since I made it to Fable Island and back again without falling, then she would too. But she's not having it.

"Come on, Theo," I say, urging her up the steep and narrow grade. "It's not that much farther. Don't look down. Keep your headlamp pointed forward so we can see where we're going."

"I can't do it," she wails. "I can't see the other side."

"You're not really on a bridge," I explain. "You think you're on a bridge..."

"Shut up, Meg," she cries.

"Technically, it's about perception. But that's for another time. First, we get there. One step at a time," I offer, tightening the straps on my pack. It's filled with two reusable water bottles, a roll of toilet paper, peanut butter crackers, Band-Aids, antiseptic cream, matches, wax paper sandwich bags for trash, extra socks, a windbreaker, a pencil case, and my black-and-white composition notebook. I wanted to bring *Fable Island* with me in case I needed the book for reference, but after I told Georgia what happened to the textbooks, she insisted on keeping it with her. Wrapping her arms around the soiled book, she cried and said she wouldn't know what would become of her if it was lost. She didn't cry like that for fear Theo and I might become lost and never come back when we stepped onto the bridge and took off across the dark open water.

Theo stumbles and I turn to look behind me. "You're doing great. We're almost there. Keep pointing the headlamp out in front so I can see."

The light goes left and then immediately swings right. "Why are we still climbing?" she wheezes.

"First we have to go up and then we'll go down."

"This is impossible. We've been going up for like an hour and a half," she says, waving her digital watch in the air. "How much longer?"

I look up, but without a single star or the moon visible it's impossible to see where we are. "You can't trust the clock."

She coughs. "I think we're in the clouds. I'm cold."

"It'll be faster going down."

Theo coughs again. "It's getting hard to breathe."

"We're high but we're not that high, Theo," I explain. "We're not so high that we're going to need oxygen."

"You might not need oxygen, Meg, but I feel like I do." She turns to the side of the bridge. "I'm dizzy."

"I didn't have this problem," I explain. "Do you want to turn around and go back?"

"I don't know."

"It's impossible in the dark to see where we are, but I don't think the bridge is any higher this time," I try. "OK. Maybe a little higher. We've been climbing for a while now haven't we?"

"I told you," she whimpers, leaning over the side of the bridge and vomiting.

I pull back her hair to hold it away from her face. "This is not what I had in mind," I admit. "This is bad." I tighten my grip on her blowing hair and whisper, "I promise we'll be on solid ground soon."

Reaching into the side pocket of my pack and pulling out the smashed roll of toilet paper, I hand Theo a wad, and she shudders. "You never told me about the cold."

"No," I answer carefully. "I didn't know. But I think you're bringing your own experience. I wasn't afraid while crossing the bridge. I wasn't even nervous. I was..." I say, thinking of the right word. "I was hopeful."

She blows her nose. "Then why is it like this for me?"

"I think you're meeting a fear," I explain, returning the roll of toilet paper to the pack and grabbing her by the hand. "But maybe when we get to the island, the island won't be ugly. Maybe that was my fear. Maybe you'll bring your perceptions and..." Theo's hand slips from mine and she sits. "What are you doing?" I shout, reaching for her. "Don't sit, Theo!"

"I can't do it. My toes are numb. And I keep slipping. I should've worn boots."

"Here, let me take your pack," I try, pulling it off her shoulders and strapping it onto the front of me. It, too, is filled with Georgia's provisions. Adding the weight of her pack to mine isn't terrible, but neither is it great. I take a deep breath and let it out slowly. "You can do this," I promise.

"No, I can't."

"You have to, Theo. You have to take me..."

"But you just said you're taking me."

"Did I? No. I meant you and I..."

"No one is going to be there, Meg. And then what? This was a mistake."

"You wanted to come," I shout. "You can't flake out now!"

"I can't do it."

"Take my hand and I'll help you."

Theo lifts her head and shines the headlamp into my eyes. "You're going to walk backward?"

With one hand on the handrail and the other in hers, I blink. "It's the only way."

"But what if you fall?"

"I won't," I assure her. "Come on. First one step and then the other. Just don't look down. We're almost at the top. Try reasoning with the fear. Tell the fear you've got this. That you're with your best friend. Tell the fear that your best friend knows the way."

"Do you? You said we're on a different bridge."

"I said it was possibly higher..."

"Then we're on a different bridge."

I pause for a moment to consider this while Theo continues shining the headlamp into my eyes. "Look down."

"But you told me not to look down."

"Then just don't shine the light into my eyes."

"Are we on a different bridge?" she cries.

"I don't know. I can't see."

"Then how do you know how long it will take to get there?"

"Stop panicking," I shout.

"You don't know, do you?"

"I don't," I concede. "Come on. Tilt the headlamp onto those boards so I can see where we're going." Now that I am beginning to think this is a different bridge, it has suddenly become a different bridge. It is not the iron bridge we were on earlier but one with slippery well-trodden wooden boards suspended from two worn ropes.

"Were's Peter?" Theo asks nervously. "I thought Georgia said..."

"I don't understand that part," I admit. "I haven't seen him. Why isn't he here for you?"

"You're the one who is supposed to know everything about Fable Island."

Do I? I think. I only know what Prof. Yardley wrote in his book and a few of the observations my mother and my grandmothers made. And of course, there is Sir Barrie's experience as he described it in his storybook. "I think the island changes for whoever visits it," I offer.

"Is that why you think Peter exists? Because Sir Barrie saw him? Only he didn't see him the same way your mom saw him?"

"Yes! I think I'm beginning to figure it out," I admit. "And your experience could be different from mine. I don't think we're going to know what will happen until we get there."

Theo cries, "You promised me poppies."

"I know, but I'm thinking we shouldn't have expectations. We might be disappointed."

"But you said…"

"Don't be frightened. We're bending time, remember?" I pull her up onto her feet. "Your shoes are wet so make sure you follow my lead. It will be like crossing a creek. Watch where I place my feet and carefully step on the boards I stepped on."

"They look dangerous."

"Just do what I tell you to do and you'll be OK."

"But what if you step on a rotten plank and you fall? Then I'm not going to do what you tell me to do."

"OK. Fair enough. If I fall, don't follow me."

As the climb over the bridge continues, I realize I'm not cold or nauseous, but Theo continues to retch every few steps. Soon, she is coughing up only slimy spit onto her stained canvas shoes. She's so exhausted she can no longer lean over the side of the bridge. Admitting defeat, I look at her and apologize. "I think we should retreat. I wasn't prepared for it to be like this. And the bridge…it's wrong."

"You said it's not real, Meg," she shudders, dropping to one knee. The bridge swings first one way and then the other.

I hold onto the rope handrails with all my strength for fear we might fall. "I know I did, but you're not well. Let's turn around."

"I'm seeing things," she admits.

"Like what?!"

"Just over there."

"Where?"

"Look up, Meg. On the other side of the bridge. It's beautiful! The sun is coming up over the island."

"There they are!" I shout as the island comes into view. "You did it, Theo! Look at the field of poppies!"

At the top of the bridge, Theo sits back on her heels and wheezes. "That was fucked."

"But we did it!" I shout.

"We still have to get down the other side."

"That's the easy part."

"Let me just sit for a minute. I don't know..."

"No! We can't stay here. What if it all changes?"

"I'm sitting," she says, looking up at me. More forlorn than I have ever seen her, Theo's eyes are rimmed with tears and she covers her face with her hands.

"Are you crying?"

"Maybe."

"I'm sorry," I offer, carefully kneeling beside her as the narrow jungle-like bridge continues to swing. "I wanted to turn around, but aren't you glad we didn't?"

"Yes," she admits.

"I knew you could do it."

She smiles weakly and blows her nose again. "I did it for Poppy."

"And look what you made," I exclaim. "So many poppies!"

She shakes her head. "I wish she could see this." I'm so anxious to get off the bridge and straight into someplace happy, but Theo is sad. "I wanted to know her," she says. "I wish she didn't die."

I turn away and look out across the island at the larger-than-life fir trees. They are like illustrated specimens, distinct and exact as if drawn to perfection with midnight green ink. "I'm not sure she did," I respond.

"I held her body, Meg."

"I know. I'm sorry. I know it's bad. I know you're getting help."

"Who told you that?"

"Your mom told Georgia and she told me."

Theo is confident when she says, "It's not a bad thing."

"I didn't say it was."

"Maybe if you'd talked to someone after your mom died, you would've felt better. It got scary, Meg. Especially when we got to middle school. Remember? You started acting weird and talking to yourself. If it wasn't for me you wouldn't have had any friends. I was the only one who loved you when everyone else was afraid…"

"You're right," I admit, watching a golden rainbow slowly arch over the island and across the lapis-colored water. "If it wasn't for you I'd be stuck with the other island. I wouldn't be seeing this one."

Theo glances down. "Oh holy mother of God, help me."

"Don't look down."

"I can't help it. How are we going to get off this thing?"

"Carefully."

"But you're glad we're here?" she asks, watching the golden rainbow as it comes into full focus and illuminates the island. "You're glad I came with you?"

"I don't know yet," I say truthfully. "I'm just glad I'm not alone."

She smiles. "Me too, Meg. I'm glad we have each other."

We look out over the verdant land. It's not hard to see where Sir Barrie found his inspiration. Maybe if we wanted to see palm trees and a volcano, we would, but we don't. It does look magical though. I peer down at one of several sapphire blue coves with its pristine white sand beach, and pray we don't encounter pirates. "It's not real, Theo," I remind her, laughing.

She shakes her head. "Then why are we going?"

"I'll explain it all later. But I do have one request. Don't imagine you're here. Believe that you're here."

"I just want to get off the bridge," she says frightened.

"We're not in a make-believe story."

"Whatever," she says annoyed.

"I mean it. Peter Pan exists."

"I'm going to have to see him again and then I'll ask him, 'Do you exist or are you make-believe?' Do you think he'll say he's make-believe?"

"Maybe he doesn't know the difference?"

Theo throws an arm into the air. "Help me up."

I reach out my hand and look her in the eye. "Promise me. To keep it safe, and to ensure we get home, we have to believe."

"I know about that part," she says as if it's obvious.

"OK. That's all I'm asking. We're stepping through another veil. And Peter Pan exists because someone long, long, long ago," I explain, "created Peter. I think he was created before Prof. Yardley saw him. Before any of the Darling women who came over the bridge saw him. Before Sir Barrie came here and saw him. And because he exists we will be able to see him too."

"How?"

"Everything that was ever created exists as an energy. And thoughts," I try, "exist as a kind of energetic pattern. So if energy doesn't die then thoughts can't die."

Theo is silent, thinking, before she responds, "Who told you that?"

I smile. "Ms. Park."

"And you believe her?"

I look out across the tops of the trees for any sign of Peter. "I do. I think we're in the process of stepping through time, where all thoughts and energies coexist."

"Is that the same thing as bending time?"

"Almost," I offer. With my hand in hers, we slowly take another step. "Dad once told me that *Peter Pan* wasn't a story about make-believe, but rather a story about the possibility of shifting time. Which is the same thing as shifting our perception." Theo looks down at her feet and nods. "But I didn't understand him. How could I? I hadn't read anything about theoretical physics. I wasn't old enough to understand how science interprets reality. I didn't understand the optics."

"Keep walking, Meg. Less talking. We need to get off the bridge then you can show me what you mean."

"Sorry," I whisper. Together we take another step. "Are you good? Do you want me to go faster?"

"No."

"When we get there what are you going to remember?" I ask.

"I'm going to remember to text Mom and tell her..."

"You're not going to text your mom!" I shout. "And besides, there's no cell service."

"But I promised her I would be home for dinner. I need to tell her I'm staying over." She laughs. "For lasagna."

"Theo!" I cry. "What were you thinking? Now she's going to call Georgia when you don't come home. How is she going to explain where we are?"

"You should've thought of that," says Theo easily.

"You should have texted your mom before we left."

"I forgot."

"Now we're screwed."

"No, we're not," she answers. "This is going to be fun."

"Not if your mom finds out. She won't believe and she'll ruin everything."

Theo pauses and looks out over the island. From this perspective, it looks like we're almost as high as a small airplane tracking just below the clouds. I've never been on a plane, but I imagine this is what it would feel like. No wonder Theo is sick. "How are you doing?" I ask.

"Not so good."

"Maybe I should carry you."

"You wouldn't be able to lift me."

"I could try..."

"If only I had wings," she says laughing, "Then I could fly!"

I smile uneasily. "Yeah, I know. We were supposed to get wings." Theo stumbles and I quickly grab her arm.

"Remember when Georgia wrote down all those instructions? It was a list of things for you to do if you ever got here."

I look at her, concerned. "No."

"You were always asking her about it so she gave you this list--THINGS TO DO WHEN YOU GET TO FABLE ISLAND."

I turn to look behind me, but we're nowhere near the end of the bridge. "I don't remember. Why didn't she give us the list before we left?"

"It was basic survival stuff. Like if you got lost and had to find your way home. Kid stuff. Remember when you used to carry that compass with you everywhere you went? In case you needed it on the island?" She shakes her head and laughs. "Stuff only Georgia would make you do."

"No, I don't remember."

"I do."

"Well, we're not going to need a compass."

"Yeah. Georgia would have packed one if she thought..."

"But she's never been here," I realize, "so how would she even know?"

Theo falters. "Let's just get down. We can figure it out as we go."

"Right," I agree. But secretly I'm not so sure. We didn't think this through. Georgia hastily packed our backpacks as though we were only going for a day hike. What if we stay here longer than that?

The trek down the other side of the swinging bridge is long and tedious and Theo continues to struggle. "We're going into an unknown, Theo," I explain. "Anything could happen. We may or may not get back in a day."

"I know."

"Are you sure you're OK?"

She nods. "I just want off."

"Are you going to be OK when we have to go home? What if…"

She deadpans. "We'll cross that bridge when we come to it."

"You're OK," I say laughing.

"That's what Dad says all the time. He's not much of a planner. Drives Mom crazy."

"But now that they're divorced, are things better at home?"

"He blames Mom for everything. She's heartbroken. I know it's not her fault, but then again…" says Theo, pausing.

"Are you saying it was her fault?"

"No. Yes. Maybe. She was lucky she didn't die. She lost so much blood, Meg." Theo stops and looks out over the island. She points to a large green bird flying over the beach and then watches it until it disappears. "I don't know what happened. But I saw her fall on the ice the day before. She didn't admit it when I asked her about it. But things went south after that."

I look for the bird, but I don't see it. "Why wouldn't she admit that she had fallen?"

"Stubborn," answers Theo. "She's wicked determined. Doesn't want people thinking she's weak."

"She's really thin."

"Yeah," says Theo, "but she's seeing someone about it now. She ate a ton while she was pregnant."

"I'm sorry," I offer. "I know you're sad."

"It's so damn frustrating. I wanted Poppy." She takes another step and wheezes. "I wanted a sister."

"You have me!"

Theo tightens her grip and squeezes my hand hard, and at this moment I realize I'm afraid for her. She doesn't have a plan. Neither do I, but I'm not scared. I'll figure it out. "You're going off to college."

"No. I'll never get in."

Theo pushes herself forward. "I wish you weren't, but I know you will."

"No," I explain. "I want something different."

She looks up and gasps. "Meg! Look! There he is! Just behind you." I turn around. "Other side!" she shouts, looking just past my shoulder. "You're not real, are you, Peter?" It looks like she's talking to herself. "You are?! Ha! He says he's real, Meg."

I throw out my hand hoping Peter will grab onto it and help us off the bridge. "Are you here?" I shout. "Where are you?"

Theo laughs. "He's right there, Meg. Right next to you."

"I don't see him."

"Well, he's right here. Real," she says satisfied.

"Are you sure? Ask him why I can't see him."

"Do I believe that I can fly?" she asks, continuing to look over my shoulder. "Now? Right now?"

I turn in a circle to face...nothing. "Theo, what are you doing?"

"Look! I have wings," she says, turning around to show me.

"No, you don't."

"But I do," she sings. "Just like you!"

"Theo!" I shout.

"You have them too, Meg. I promise." I turn around but I don't see anything. "Come on," she says, taking my hand in hers. "I want off and Peter says we can fly."

"Theo, no, no, no," I plead, pulling her back. "You can't fly."

She laughs. "Peter says you've forgotten who you are."

"Shit. Don't scare me, Theo."

"He says you need to believe."

"But I do," I try.

She shakes her head. "Nope. Not like you're supposed to believe. Come on, Meg. He's here. Just like you said."

"I never said..."

"He says you're being too logical." She laughs. "You're the one who wanted this, Meg. The one who wore those pink faerie wings every day after your mom died. The ones Georgia made for you. Remember? Yours look just like that. Only now they're not torn."

"What's going on, Peter?" I shout. "Are you here?" No answer. I blink and the island goes in and out of focus. "I'm frightened, Theo," I whisper. "I think something's wrong."

"Come on! Peter says we can fly."

"How?"

Theo stands on the tips of her toes and looks out over the island. "He says you're not a Wendy."

"I know," I hiss. "But that's not my fault."

"He says, 'Yes it is.' "

"No, it's not," I complain. "I never had a say..."

Theo is serious. "Listen to Peter. He says everyone is a Wendy. All they have to do is remember her."

"I don't understand."

"You just have to believe."

"In what?" I shout. "Make-believe?"

"I love my wings," she coos, lifting herself onto the tips of her toes. "They're gossamer."

"Theo!" I scream. "Are you out of your mind? You're going to fall!"

And just like that she slips out from under the ropes and steps off the bridge as everything disappears in a ruptured haze of pixie dust.

Seventeen

Not a day goes by that I don't think of Theo. It's been over five years since she stepped off the bridge and flew with Peter Pan over the breaking waves and across the tops of the trees. I don't doubt she went, although there is still a part of me that is incredulous. She came home that night with a handful of translucent poppies and a dog-eared composition notebook that once belonged to my mom. Written in purple ink, the notebook is filled with Mom's drawings and descriptions of the island. Theo said Peter gave it to her. But more than that, Theo came home with a new appreciation for herself. She said she had never wanted to find Fable Island and didn't need to believe in the faeries now that she was sixteen, but she said she could trust the magic. Peter made sure of that.

When I asked her if she saw the faerie realm, she didn't answer. I don't know if it was because she didn't see it, or because she was afraid for me. Did she think I would be angry with her for going? I'm not angry. I'm glad it was her and not me. Maybe I got what I wanted from Fable Island just as she got what she wanted. And what did I need? That's a hard question to answer because over the years what I wanted always seemed to shift. Maybe I wanted the freedom to leave home and get answers to who I was. Being a descendant of four generations of Darling women has been hard to live up to. Maybe I didn't want that responsibility. Or maybe I needed my own beginning and not theirs. It's hard to say.

The tears come when I think about Theo. I wish she could have taken the joy she felt when she came home and done something big like write a book or share the stories of Fable Island all over the world, but she said she didn't know what would happen to her story if she shared it. She promised both Georgia and me that the best of times were ahead for her because she really did believe that they were. But I wanted so much more for her. She could have made her own contribution to the Darling manuscript and published it because she was the one who went to Fable Island, and not me, but she refused. She said she wasn't a writer and that if she shared her experience, it wouldn't be real. And she wanted Fable Island to be real.

We don't see each other that much anymore. When I come home for Christmas she will stop by for a brief visit to bring us one of her mother's cakes, but she doesn't stay long. I want her to sit by the fire and reminisce about that day we climbed the bridge to Fable Island together, but she says we should keep our memories our own. I know she's sad I didn't trust her, but I didn't. How could I? I didn't see the wings. I retreated and before I knew it I was back in Georgia's kitchen. I never reached the island of my dreams. Somehow I only made it to the island of my fears and that experience has made more of a lasting impression on me than anything else.

The Faeries of Fable Island remains incomplete. I know it's a book that needs to be written, that begs to be written, but I still don't feel like I'm the one who can write it. How can I? I have doubted and dismissed the island. I haven't lived up to the Darling name. But I am me, I remember, turning to the computer and hitting "submit." I close the laptop and sit back in my desk chair. The philosophy test was easy, I think, closing my eyes and recalling the days when I thought I would never get into Yale. But miraculously, I did.

Ms. Park told me not to get my hopes up. And I didn't. She told me it was a long shot, and it was. But I guess it was something Georgia said that helped me remember my past and made me truly want it after all. She said I just needed to trust and believe that a college experience could be mine. I wasn't going to hope I got in. I was going to see myself there as though I belonged, as though it was real. In my head, I imagined myself back at the top of the bridge looking out into the unknown, and from there I was able to write my college essay. It was about the faeries of Fable Island after all.

I wrote: *Too many people stand on the precipice of their desires afraid of their past, afraid of themselves, and afraid of the truth. I don't know the way forward in life. I don't have that answer. There are directions we can take, and there are mountains to climb, but the biggest mountain we climb is ourselves. Clichéd as this has become, this is my truth.*

My aunt Georgia once told me when I was young that the smartest way forward out of grief is to believe that death isn't real. It is simply a journey from one existence to another. I told myself then, as I continue to tell myself now, grief exists. It complicates the mind. It muddies perception.

I don't doubt my mother and each of my grandmothers went to Fable Island. I don't doubt that my best friend, Theo, went. And more than anything, I don't doubt that Peter Pan and the faerie realm exist. We hold onto the beliefs we do because of how we perceive them. Perhaps proving the existence of Fable Island will help lead us to an understanding and respect for this truth. I will work hard to prove that Peter Pan and the faerie realm belong to us all. They give us a playfulness and an innate curiosity about ourselves and our surroundings that can help us understand time.

Time is manufactured. I know Sir Barrie's Peter Pan is a book about time, although it's not read that way. Trapped as we are in our own linear thinking, we fear the unknown. We fear death. We fear growing up. We fear losing. But Sir Barrie understood that time can be manipulated and I do believe that one day we will be able to prove this scientifically. Time and space are interlopers that disrupt thinking. If we can respect that the world is vast and mysteriously uncertain, we will come out ahead. Time boxes us into a construct and renders us immobile. There is no shame in stopping time or failing to grow up. What exactly does it mean to grow? I understand nothing about my past as much as I understand everything. I am a fraction of who I once was and who I am becoming.

My aunt Georgia, who helped me when I was struggling to understand my deepest insecurities, reminded me of something I once said. I was probably five or six years old when she asked me, "Do you believe in faeries?" Without missing a beat I answered her, "Of course, I believe in myself." Well, I do believe in myself. After all, I am a fifth-generation Darling. Without my mother and my grandmothers, I would be lost to the sensibilities of this lore, and although we are not storybook characters, we are, in truth, forever defined by Fable Island, the sentimentality of our past, and the possibilities of our own discoveries. It is these connections we create and the possibilities we master that bring us either our loss or our joy.

Fable Island may not be real but it exists. And there is a difference. It is in the hearts and minds of those who believe. That's what the faeries would ask of us. But more than in our hearts, and more than in our minds, Fable Island exists because we believe in ourselves and the responsibility we have to this planet. We are stewards, capable of either caring for her or destroying her. The choice is ours. And should we choose light, the faeries of Fable Island will take us to our greatest desires.

———

Theo drives a school bus. She says she loves the job, the freedom she feels sitting behind the wheel, the laughter the children bring when they skip up the bus steps, and the wonder she shares with each of them about the mysteries of Peter Pan's magic. She gives each of the children a pair of gossamer wings to wear while she drives them to school. And when they arrive, and hop off the bus excited and happy, she knows this is what Fable Island will always mean to her. I have to remind myself that her experience and mine will be our own. Peter Pan has made sure of that.

I will be graduating from college in two months. Imagine that?! But then what? I don't know. I will go home for a while to help Georgia pack up the house. She's devastated about moving, but we both know it's for the best. She can't afford to stay. Grandad's antique books that once sat in a cardboard box waiting to be sold will never bring in enough money to pay the taxes. We don't know if they were really ever worth anything. Maybe Grandad told us they were priceless because, to him, the books held great sentimental value. After all, each of the books once belonged to his daughter. My mom. On the title page of the various illustrated copies of *Peter Pan,* she had written her name, Wendy M. Darling, in a childish scrolling hand, next to her mother, her mother, and her mother's large looping letters.

As much as I was desperate to leave these childhood memories behind, it is these memories that shaped me and are pushing me to return. I don't know how we'll do this going forward, or how Georgia will find her footing once she leaves. After all that Georgia has done for me and all that she has sacrificed and endured, I wish I could help her with the expenses so she could stay. But with a degree in philosophy, I'm not going to be making that kind of money anytime soon. I pause and consider something I had pushed away long ago. If Sir Barrie could write a book about Fable Island that became world-famous, sold in the millions, and was turned into stage plays, musicals, and movies, then why can't I? Why shouldn't I share the mysteries of time? I never thought of myself as a writer, but maybe when you're writing your truth you don't need to think. You write what is.

I open the laptop and let my hands linger. In my mind, I can see my dad, now frail and slumped over in his rattan chair. His wife is by his side, and together they stare self-consciously into the computer camera. She puts a slender dark hand on his shoulder and smiles. She rarely speaks. My dad looks content and I'm glad he sought medical care for his liver. He won't live forever. I know that. But at least he didn't give up. I touch the keyboard and it is as if the keys and the words and my voice speak to this long sought-after story inside each of the Darling women. We do have a story to tell. And it doesn't belong to anyone but us, the women who traveled to Fable Island and kept the truth hidden. Until now.

I pull out my dog-eared copy of *Fable Island* and open it up to page seventy-two. I no longer wear the gloves now that the book is stained and worn. I told Georgia this is how I want it to be. I want it to remain old and read and loved so she never had the book cleaned or reappraised. I peel back several pages that are stuck together and read, *We are organisms living in the past, but will we ever know what the past really is? Is this past something we need it to be, or will the way open without needing the past? Think about the way forward and we forget the past. Return to the past and the future is lost. There is nothing of time. It is not real.* "But it exists," I whisper.

I return to the computer and e-mail my dad. *Hi. I know I'm long past the age of going to Fable Island, but do you think it's still possible? I mean, what if I try again? My birthday's coming up in a few days. What if I went home and tried again? Would you say a prayer for me that I make it this time? I would love to come out and see you.*

I'd have to fly. Argh! You know how I don't want to do that (smiling emoji), but maybe I will find my wings and make the trip.

I can't help but smile when I think about the faerie wings Georgia made for me after Mom died. I wore them until they became torn and shredded into unrecognizable bits. Instinctively, I turn to look behind me and it is as though time has circled back around and I am six years old again. I can't help but laugh. It's a genuine belly laugh, the first in such a long, long time. I am truly wearing a pair of pink faerie wings. My mom may be gone, but she has never left me.

I return to the keyboard, and with trembling fingers I type, *Maybe I didn't need to spend all this time looking for my wings, Dad. Maybe I had them all along. Maybe I really can fly. And maybe it's time I found the truth of Fable Island.*

Yours etc., Megan Elida Fay

Acknowledgments

Fable Island is as much a mythical place as anything real. Crafted from the mind, it is a place of fantasy. But do we not live in a fantasy of our own making? This can happen when we are troubled and imagining some altered version of the truth. I have Susie Miller to thank for introducing me to the notion that our minds create our reality. When the mind falters any number of mythological experiences can happen.

Writing *The Faeries of Fable Island* has been an initiation of sorts, where my entire self-worth has been laid out on the page for you to examine. We can create beautiful lives for ourselves by believing we have the power within us to trust grief and allow it to pass through as it must. If we fail to honor grief and sweep it under the rug in the hope that it goes away, we can't work our way free of it. By honoring those who have been a part of my past, my present, and my future, I honor myself.

Marsha Stultz, thank you for helping me honor my writer's voice so that I could find the words I needed to write this story.

Thank you, Deeda Burgess, Suzanne Astolfi, Gaetan Davis, Carson Davis, Steve Davis, Matthea Daughtry, Hallie Daughtry, Steve Tibbetts, Nowell Stoddard, and those, too numerous to mention, from the Maine Coast Waldorf School who contributed to this story. Your friendship and encouragement have meant so much to me over the years. Without you, this book would not have been possible.

My heartfelt thanks to my daughters Sarah and Lydia, and my former husband, Rob, for giving me the space and the place and the way to seek this writer's life even if it meant I was, at times, distracted from you. I love you.

To Adam and Adrian, you are so loved and welcomed into this family. Thank you for showering your unwavering love on my daughters and my grandchildren.

Thank you, Janet, David, Caroline, and Meredith Rivard. It takes a village.

Thank you, Berry Manter, for contributing to the magic of this story.

To Winslow McCagg, thank you for sharing beautiful notions about landscape and place.

To my editor Lee Bumsted, not the first to edit this book, but happily the last, for providing a steady hand when it became too difficult for me to parse out this prose. I am indebted to you and all that you desire—you are as much a part of this quest to make beautiful books as I am. Thank you.

Emily Kallick, once again, thank you for your beautiful vision and un-wavering optimism. Many hands and many hearts are coming along on this publishing journey, and you are, undeniably, my right hand.

Thank you, J. Felice Boucher, for bringing more beauty than I could ever imagine to this book cover. I am forever grateful.

To all those who read, comment on, and share my books, thank you. May your light be the light of happiness.

Read on for an excerpt from
RESTLESS

"A lyrical historical novella about an elusive young Parisian woman who flees from her family and romantic relation-ships...A brief but memorable tale with prose that sings."
- Kirkus Reviews -

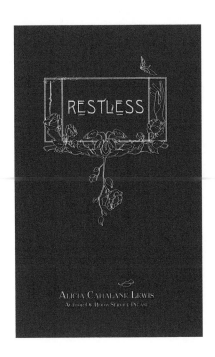

Restless

One

Emilie

There is nothing to be afraid of. Love is a stereoscope of emotional pictures in the mind. And the mind, rummaging around and through love, complicates the heart. And then the heart cries. It weeps. Love is a complex set of emotions I never thought I would be able to understand, that is until I met you.

———

I do not normally engage in conversations I feel threatened by. I pull out of situations that make me uncomfortable. I do not react well to strangers, and because you are perceived to be a stranger I feel noticeably unhinged by your presence.

The boulevard is dotted with dappled light. You come to me in this abstract way, the whole of you invisible until I lift my eyes and gaze upon your battered soul. You hide behind a waistcoat, your breast a peacock blue, and I notice that the gold pocket watch is neither elaborate nor sentimental. This mystifies me. You walk upright, as fashionable men walk in the early evening, with your top hat securely in place, and neither my sorry eyes nor my threadbare skirt diverts the gaze you have upon these wilted flowers. It is the flowers you want. I am no one. My skirt is unfashionable thereby making me a vagabond and you, the reason I must live.

———————

The streets of Paris are antiquated, although there are new electric lamps on the Avenue de l'Opéra to liven the dreary moods of those who live inside her columned vestibules. But I am not certain you are as well-heeled as your polished boots make you appear to be, and I wonder now if your vestibule has columns. I know mine did. Once.

I walk behind you, your gloved hand smartly carrying a bouquet of unopened roses, and I follow the shadows your feet make on the cobblestone street as you sidestep horse manure and mud. My hallowed boots are cracked and absorb smells. I once walked in puddles and disregarded it all. Until now. I remember to be careful where I place my feet. Careful, so that should you invite me in to dine with you I will be clean. I have nowhere to go. I once had a fashionable house, a maman, and a papa who brought me sweetness, and there was nothing to ever want. I am no longer that child, for I ran away from this long ago. I now have needs.

I notice the stained glass window, now cracked, and you notice perhaps the tarnished handle of your apartment door, but you do not look up at the glass as you enter. Your gloved hand, covered smartly in gray felt, is ever so slightly stained. You seem to appreciate the sudden warmth, but you struggle to close the wooden door against the wind. And it is in this moment that you lift your dark eyes, diverted momentarily from the pleasures of your room, to look at me. I thought I had been long gone from a realm such as this, but should you invite me in to dine I would hold a silver spoon and sip my soup just as you do.

———————

It never occurs to me that you might have a wife. After all, there are roses. Red. I struggle against the darkening day. I have nowhere promising to go. I could turn and run, as I am inclined to, and push my narrow boots across an abstraction such as this life. I could promise myself nothing, and believe in nothing, but nothing is as complicated as something. I know I should have taken the taffy Papa gave me and enjoyed its sweetness, but I turned on him as I must turn on you.

I am no longer a child. I know nothing a child knows. I have my memories, but they are incomplete vestiges of a bygone era when I was taken around the pebbled parks of Paris in a barouche so we could be seen. My maman sat upon stiff brocade and I, tipped in mink from head to toe, sat stoically stone-faced. There is no other recourse, but a memory, for Maman and Papa died and have long ago been buried. I have outgrown my past and have thrown the tattered aubergine wool coat and hat, a fashionable child's bonnet, away. I turned on my brother Henri and tossed my wealth aside when what I had was way too much.

Do I make myself and the picture postcards of my life clear? I grew up in want of nothing. I would come in from a windy walk such as this, my blonde hair curled and tied up in ribbons, my boots polished, and be greeted at the door. I entertained myself by a fire such as you are going to do. Where is your man to answer the door? Have you a wife?

You stop momentarily when you look upon me and gasp. I am a heathen for sure, but I am old enough to know I can get away with this childlike innocence. I push the fraying cap off my head to show you the golden stubble of lopped-off curls. I give all that is left of the curls to the winter wind so that the lamp will show you just how my gold beckons. There are some who move their feet as though in all of life there is a dance. I move my tousled hair in ways I imagine those who have taken to the prairie move theirs. At least I feel that their lives should afford them tousled hair and wind.

I once saw a picture postcard of the American West and imagined myself living there. I wanted to roll up the sleeves of my dirty muslin, take off my sunbonnet, and let the wind carry me as a tumbleweed across my unintended existence. In the West, I would have a maman, a papa, and a brother who would pioneer their rugged souls alongside mine. We would travel as a brave and studious family into uncharted realms. We would go where no one had dared to go before, conquering our fear of rattlesnakes and vermin.

There is nothing easy about the windy streets of Paris, especially at night. I toss what is left of my tangled hair and you grimace. You close the door and now you are behind a panel I cannot see into or through. There are curtains at your apartment window, perhaps double-lined to protect you from the cold. I wear a soiled but once-opulent gentleman's dark opera cape and a pair of mismatched riding gloves. If you were foolish enough to drop a glove, and I know not if one of these was yours (as much as I would love for it to be), I was clever enough to pick it up. I have a smart collection of misplaced gloves: dark leather, flannel, silk, suede, fingerless, frayed woolen mittens, and a child's lavender kidskin with a single pearl button. Extremely rare.

I run my hands down the shrunken summer skirt of dusty rose and tug on the parcel to make sure my gloves are still there. I wear a tattered wool petticoat for warmth in the winter and carry it in the silk parcel in the summer, but the mismatched gloves have become something of a talisman. I feel as though I must carry them with me, always, for protection. I pull uneasily on the soiled skirt, and despite the cold sharp air, I unbutton the fraying collar of my flannel shirtwaist. It will not suit in a few months. I have grown and begun to fill out. My hips are not as narrow and my breasts are not as lean.

The wind carries with it the scent of something newly cut crackling on a vigorous fire. There are wet branches of some kind that you have tossed, without thinking, and they smoke. I hear you cough. I strain to listen for the pitter-patter of children's feet, the chime of a grandfather clock announcing the hour, and a bell to tell you it is time to dress for dinner, but the house is quiet. I cannot imagine a wife. I feel it in every part of my being that I am yours and when I knock upon the door, and you answer, you will lock your wondrous eyes upon mine and then in all seriousness complain that I am too modern and must never go about the streets alone. You will take me into your arms, hold me against your heart, and I will soften and promise you I have no need for independence.

The wind shifts direction and brings with it a frozen spitting rain. I am without an umbrella, or anything, really, to divert the misery. But this is what I know: I am orphaned. I haven't a warm fire to go home to. I once had these pleasures, but they are now lost. I pause and stare into the crimson light that bleeds profusely from behind the open curtains. They are red. The papered walls are red. Your wife loves red. Or is it your mother? I have a hard time imagining that you have decorated your apartment yourself, but one never knows these days. We are between knowing.

Uneasily, you close the curtains. I can only imagine your tall trim body, your slender hand on the varnished fireplace mantle, and a nod to your lover behind this veil, for the dusty curtains are too thick to make your movements known to me. I must imagine. You are a gentleman to buy my flowers. And when you took them from me you never once looked into me as I looked into you. You put the centime into my frozen hand and watched the petals bend. I know you wanted to protect them for the someone you love, and so when you turned from me I followed. I want to know your love.

The streets are busy now with evening travelers and I am getting kicked about with mud from the wheels of their horse-drawn carriages. I hesitate to leave you, for if I do, and turn my back, I know I will wound myself once more. I was born to greater wealth than you. I lost it. I could have found perhaps temporary comfort with my aunt Élodie, but she was cruel, or so I thought. I had read too many harrowing tales of cruelty, and I knew that once she took Maman's money, as all vain aunts are want to do, especially in the stories I had read, she would throw me out upon the grate. So to spare her the newfound richness of her grieving heart, or is that the poverty, I stole away into the night and never said goodbye.

I am sure Henri was sent to live in an impoverished house for wayward souls and had I stayed with him I would have accompanied him. Or I would have been sent away to school, and given a uniform and a matching coat. Or taken into another home and given perfectly harmless chores to do. I know not. Had I not run from home would we have met some other way?

I have dreamt of this life. In it, I am sitting by an electric lamp taking stock of all I am. I do not want. I have a fire. Your love. We have a child. Had I stayed with my brother who knows where I would be? Perhaps my aunt would have taken pity on us and let us stay with her in Maman's great house. She would have employed an even finer governess and dressed us up in her gaudy ways. But the house was sold, and I am certain my brother was stripped of his name and shipped off, and I, as a result of my childish ways, have been left behind to walk the streets alone.

In my mind, my brother is somewhere just as negligible as these windy streets, but I do not know. I know nothing of his whereabouts, and over time, as I have grown accustomed to myself I fear that should I ever see him I would find him changed. I would not know him and he would not know me. No face of his would look familiar for he was but four years old and I, eleven, when our maman and papa were taken to their God.

In her spectacular demise of character, yes quite a character flaw, my feral aunt, once suited for a lesser rung, now wears my mother's diamond brooch. I have seen her parade about the streets dragged down by Maman's mink, but there is nothing I can do about it. She abandoned me at the time I needed her most. I do not want her or my mother's jewels. I do not need her fur. I close the stolen cape around me tightly, and in doing so remember Maman, but it is not a happy memory. I never understood nor will I ever understand her love. I know I confused her. No, let me be more clear. I compounded the fears she had about herself and there is nothing more to say. She did not want children. She preferred the scene to be something of another silhouette where men are lovers uninterrupted by impatient child-ish squeals.

When it was hers to take, Maman took her mother's money and spent it freely. Against Papa's wishes, she gambled at roulette and won enough to buy a house so that before I was brought into this world she became known for her great wealth. She hid the gambling.

It is my late mother's riches, she would say, and no one suspected the truth. But I knew. Papa was beside himself with guilt and anguished greatly.

Servants talk, he would whisper, then tie his silk tie tighter and do nothing about it, too weak or ineffectual, I guess, to go against her.

For this, I find him just as cruel. How does an eager man become weak? And how, I fear, will I ever understand Maman's penchant for more? Had she been found out, no one would have accepted us in that inner circle of old wealth. She would have been thrown to the street to scavenge. But before she was found to be a fraud, as I am certain as fleas in my bed that she would have been, Maman and Papa died in a train car accident. I have come to the streets of Paris a pauper with her secret still intact.

I made the choice to flee. I look back on this time and it is as clear as glass. There are no irregular shadows. I see the vibrancy of the moonlit night and the golden lamps upon the street just as I did the night I ran away. I still walk the avenues and beg. I steal. I take what is mine to take and offer whatever I can in its place. Perhaps some part of me wanted to know the streets the way a gypsy knows the streets, and so as one of those wayward characters in Maman's novels, I took her to the streets to know. I guess you could say I wanted what I could not have just as Maman wanted what was beyond her reach. She put on a costume, her diamonds and pearls, just as I have put on a costume, my frayed cap and cape, and together our diverted souls walk the streets of Paris begging to find whatever it is that has gone missing.

It occurs to me that if I knock on your door you will either turn me away or take me in. I have nothing to lose for calling upon you. I turn the idea over, step away from the iron gate in fear, but then lower my eyes, and take hold of the latch. Without further hesitation, I throw it open.

I will love you, I promise. I feel it. My heart beats erratically as though Maman has stepped in front of me and warned me against this, for in her mind I am lost to finer things. I deserve my station. The wind rattles the gate and it swings away from me. These are unusual feelings. I know not if it is my nerves or if I am cold. I hide my parcel of mismatched gloves in the shrubbery and smooth my skirt with my trembling hands. I tiptoe up the stone steps. It is beyond my dignity to turn. I must see you. I know of no other feeling, like this, at this moment. I am expecting the look on your face to be unpleasant, but I will explain who I am and why I am here.

The night air is getting sharp, the wind bitter. I have a grate to go to, but it is crowded. There are too many souls who come to Paris to scavenge about. And what is it that they hope to find? There are broken bottles, bits of soiled ticking, and a lost doll, but these are never enough. Yet they should be more than enough. Shouldn't they? How is it then that I want more? I continue to stumble up the steps and run a torn glove down my tear-stained face. I cannot deem Maman irresponsible, I realize, just because she wanted diamonds. We want what we want.

I stand upon the stoop and turn the brass bell. It, too, is in need of polishing. All at once, you are frozen in time. I feel you belong to me and I touch the bell once more. I know not how, but when your hand touched mine our lives entwined. Are we not destined to encircle one another? The door opens and you stand erect, your shoulders taut. There is unease. I have interrupted your evening meal. I turn to look beyond the vestibule but your house has neither columns nor a soaring ceiling. You are alone. There is a fire. I take a step toward you and you brush me away. I see that you have placed the crushed roses in a slim porcelain vase, but the lonely buds droop. The warm water has not yet revived them.

Did you know I stole those? Je les ai volé, I want to say. I needed a centime for something to eat. If you suspect that you have brought home stolen goods will you throw them out or will you continue to pry them open? Warm water should do the trick and I think about asking you for a warm bath but it is all too much, and just as you are about to close the door on me I turn from you and run. I fly as fast as I can down the slippery steps and through the swinging gate. Into the night I dash, forever haunted by your touch.

Continue reading
Restless by Alicia Cahalane Lewis
tatteredscript.com